TABLE

Written with Daniel C. McCarthy
The devil comes to collect from a man
who sold his soul for the taste of success.

THE WRITER

"Again?" my wife asked as she peeked over my shoulder at the umpteenth rejection letter from another publisher. "It's not like I'm surprised. I don't want to say I told you so, but I told you so."

"How about some support here? Knock off the negativity. Rejections are part of the process."

"What can be positive about a transcript marked in red like a bloody battlefield? Give it up. Find another hobby."

Trying to tune out my wife, I continued skimming the editor's comments.

"Your story stinks," she whined. "Why bother making changes? It'll never sell. You don't know what the hell you're doing."

"How wrong you are. I'm so close. Most editors decide in five minutes if what took a year to write is publishable. This editor critiqued all four hundred pages of my manuscript and made a handful of suggestions to improve the story. She'll collaborate with me if I revise and resubmit."

"And wait for another rejection?"

I slammed my fist on the table. "Dammit. Don't you get it?"

"I get it. If your writing wasn't so crappy, you wouldn't need to depend on someone else to fix your mess."

"You have no clue what I've gone through to write this novel. I put my heart and soul into every word, then condensed it into a three-paragraph synopsis to grab the publisher's interest. This could be my ticket."

"A ticket to nowhere. There are reasons other writers become successful, and you don't."

Tired of arguing, I escaped into my office to read the critique in private. The editor loved the idea of the protagonist being a struggling author but expressed displeasure with the miserable wife introduced in chapter eighteen. In bold letters, she stated, **Why make the husband so shallow? Wimpy men who don't stand up for themselves turn off readers. Give him a backbone. Ditch the unbearable wife character. The plot would**

work much better if the story weren't so depressing.

What she said made sense. Deleting the annoying wife allows me to do a serious rewrite and improve the plot to make it more upbeat.

"And another thing!" my wife yelled as she barged into my office. "If you ask my opinion, it's a boring read and doesn't get interesting until the wife enters the story. Ditch everything before her introduction. Otherwise, you're in danger of losing the reader."

"Did I ask for your opinion?"

"I'll give it anyway, but you're too thickheaded to take advice from someone who's not a writer. I got news for you, hubby. You're no writer either."

"Why discuss this? You're always right. They name streets after you. They call them *one way*."

"An author writes what they know. What do you know about anything? You don't write memoirs or biographies. You write fiction. It's all bullshit, and you expect readers to believe in the mindless idiots you create. Your characters have no birth certificate, DNA, or fingerprints. They don't exist, Writer Man."

"An author's goal is to bring their characters to life and make the reader believe in them. Give them a heartbeat. Make their personalities unique and memorable."

"You're doing a lousy job. Except for the wife, your characters are one-dimensional. She's the only one with personality and a heartbeat. If you had any brains, you'd introduce her to the story sooner. Without the wife in the earlier chapters, the story drags. You need to grab the reader from page one. Don't give the reader a chance to put the book down. Because once they do, they'll never pick it up again."

"The editor suggested the opposite."

"What makes her an expert?"

"She's more qualified than you."

"I've read enough books to be an excellent judge of what works and what doesn't."

"Judge this," I said as I deleted the document from my hard drive.

Her eyes bulged. "What the hell are you doing?"

I held the only printed copy in front of her face. "My novel needs a serious rewrite." I put aside the first seventeen chapters before I fed the remaining pages through the razor-sharp blades of the paper shredder. "Any characters introduced after page one-hundred-forty-eight will disappear as if they never existed."

She screamed as the blades shredded the pages into confetti.

"This is the story, woman. When I introduced the wife in chapter eighteen, I had no plans to make her the main character. But her dominating personality took over and destroyed the plot. The nasty wife is the mindless idiot the novel can do without. How's that for a plot twist?"

She stood with her mouth open with the look of fear in her eyes.

"You are the fictional wife I created. Since you have no birth certificate, DNA, or fingerprints, you only exist on paper. As the author, I'm in control and can mold my character's personality however I want them. I also control their destinies."

"You're mad," she hollered.

"Pissed is a better word." A smile crossed my face. "Watch this. With a few keystrokes, I can make my characters laugh or cry, live, or die. In your case, I gave you an inch, and you took a mile and became a hateful witch. You, my dear, are a failed experiment. Once I destroy everything after chapter seventeen, nobody will ever know you existed because you never did."

The paper shredder chewed up the pagers as her cries grew weaker. Her image faded. With her no longer a distraction, I sat at the word processor. *Now, where was I? Oh yeah, chapter eighteen.*

1942

Another small turnout gathered at the Nighthawk Cafe. Phil wondered if his business or the nation would ever return to how it was. So many of his customers were overseas defending the country. Because of the trying times, nobody was in the mood to mingle. Tonight, only three people occupied Phil's Cafe.

A middle-aged gentleman wearing a blue suit sat alone as he nursed his coffee. On the opposite side of the counter sat thug Frankie Collins, alongside a statuesque redhead. Phil watched from a distance as Collins waggled his finger in her face. His attractive companion with bloodshot eyes looked dejected as Frankie did the talking.

Not one to pry, Phil continued with his usual routine, waiting for Edward R. Murrow's report about the Allies' progress in the war. He sifted through the annoying static and caught the tail end of the radio broadcast from the Glen Island Casino. The program ended with a swinging rendition of the Glenn Miller song, *In the Mood.* Seconds later came Murrow's familiar introduction. "This ... is England."

Semi-regular, Henry Walters strolled in and tossed a quarter on the counter. "Hey, Phil. Gimmie change for the payphone on the corner. A dime and three nickels will do."

Phil hurried with the exchange to return to the broadcast.

Henry looked around. "Where is everybody? It's Friday night."

"Where do you think they are? There's a war going on."

Henry pointed with his chin toward the couple sitting in the corner. "Who's the good-looking dame with Frankie Collins?"

"Never saw her before."

"Collins is bad news. He's always up to no good."

"I know of his reputation, Henry, but he's behaving himself tonight. I need every paying customer I can get. Excuse me. I have to return to the news report."

Phil moved his ear closer to the radio.

The couple continued with their own heated debate.

"What are we doin', doll?"

"I don't know, Frankie. I.. just.. don't.. know."

"Listen, Audrey. I can't stay here all night twistin' your arm. It's late. You gonna cooperate or not?"

"I can't do this. My boss has been so helpful since my husband left to fight the Japs."

"Stop bitching. Do what I say."

"Frankie, it's wrong."

"So is adultery."

"I drank too much that night. You took advantage of me."

"You're no saint, Audrey. What you're gonna do ain't no bigger sin than the one you already committed."

Audrey wiped her moist eyes with a tissue. "It's your fault I'm in this mess."

"It takes two to tango."

"I told you to stop. You overpowered me."

"I did you a favor. You loved every minute."

"A favor? You got me pregnant."

"Who says I'm the one who knocked you up?"

"I'm not a tramp. I drifted one time." Audrey looked away and breathed out her cigarette smoke.

15

"Look at me, Sugar. Your husband won't hang around once he finds you were unfaithful while he was away."

"What you're asking me to do is criminal."

"I'm losing patience, dammit." She whimpered when he yanked a handful of her hair, pulling her closer. "Gimme what I want. Or else."

"OUCH! Let go, Frankie. You're hurting me."

The café's only other customer glanced their way.

Frankie gave the onlooker a menacing gaze. "What are you staring at, old man? What's going on over here ain't none of your damn business. Don't look in this direction again. Ya got it?"

The onlooker apologized before he focused back on the newspaper.

Frankie glanced out the window. "Hey, Phil. What's with the two uniforms that keep passing by outside? You know of anything going on?"

"They're walking their beat. Every night, like clockwork at 11:00, they stop in for their free coffee and doughnuts."

The clock said it was 10:45. Wanting to finish business before the beat officers entered the café, he turned his attention back to Audrey. "Let's move this along. This is your last chance."

"I'm scared."

"How scared will you be when your husband returns from the war? I'd love to see his reaction when he meets the new member of the family."

Audrey bit her lower lip. "Okay, okay, you win. I'll do it." She jotted numbers on the back of a matchbook cover and handed him a key.

"A deal is a deal. I'll hook you up with my guy tomorrow afternoon. He'll make the problem go away. But tonight, we'll have a little fun again. Let's call it one for the road. You don't have to worry about getting pregnant. You already are."

"I'd rather be dead than have you touch me again."

"A hell of a way to show your appreciation. My guy is expensive. I'm paying the tab. How else are you gonna reimburse me?"

"I just gave you the key and combination. The heist will more than compensate for the cost of the doctor."

"I told you earlier, you will give me what I want. You are part of the package. I want you." He yanked her arm and pulled her off the stool. "Let's go. It's time to pay up."

"Get your hands off me."

"I'll do more than put my hands on you. You got a long night ahead, and it's doubtful if you'll get much sleep."

The man who sat alone took a step toward Frankie. "You heard the lady, Collins. Get your hands off her."

"What did I tell you earlier? Mind your own business, pops? You don't wanna mess with me." Frankie gave the older man a confused look. "How the hell do you know my name?"

The stranger pulled out his badge. "Detective White. NYPD. You're under arrest."

Frankie darted toward the door. The two officers walking their beat stopped the hoodlum from going any further. One officer slapped handcuffs on his wrists. He whined, "Ya ain't got nothin' on me, copper."

"Audrey claims you were planning a robbery."

"What? It's Audrey that was planning the robbery. I tried to talk her out of it." Frankie removed the matchbook cover from his shirt pocket. "Here it is. The combination, written in her own handwriting. She wanted me to be her partner. As an incentive, she promised to be my mistress until I grew tired of her. I may be a wise guy, but I'm not a thief. I regret getting mixed up with the broad. Yeah, Audrey's a beautiful gal, but I found out too late how her conniving mind worked."

"Save your breath, Collins. We know your game. Audrey came to the precinct to report your scheme. She agreed to cooperate and help set you up. With your big mouth and mind of a sewer rat, you made it easy for us to nail you. Extortion and conspiracy to commit larceny. Now we can add attempted rape to the charges."

"I don't know the combination," Audrey said. "I made up those numbers. The key is from an old apartment building."

The detective motioned to the officers. "Take Collins downtown."

"You got no proof of nothin'. It's Audrey's word against mine. Ain't nobody gonna believe a whore."

"Thanks to Phil, police have the evidence they need. Audrey agreed to meet you here for a reason. We planted a bug under the counter where you two sat and recorded every word to reel-to-reel."

As police led him away, Frankie warned, "Wait till your husband comes home, Mommy. He'll learn what a slut you are and how you've been keeping busy while he endangered his life halfway around the world."

Audrey motioned for the officers to stop. "Hold on a minute, officers. I want him to hear this." She fought back her tears. "A day after your extortion threats began, I received a telegram. Charlie's plane went down. He's dead. Unlike you, he was a brave man."

"Ain't that a shame. You got no husband, and you're pregnant with someone else's kid."

"My child will grow up believing they were conceived during the act of love before Daddy went overseas to defend America." She reached into her purse for a Chesterfield. "You're not the father, Frankie. I've been sleeping around and was pregnant before we hooked up. I claimed the baby was yours because you knew a guy who could take care of my problem." She pointed her finger in his face. "Frankie Boy. My baby will be a better person than both of us."

The excitement was over. Whatever Phil missed in Murrow's report, he'd read about it in tomorrow's paper. As the squad car pulled away, Audrey placed the cigarette between her lips. "Got a light?"

Phil shook his head. "I don't get it."

"Get what?"

"Smoking. It wouldn't surprise me if someday it's discovered cigarettes aren't good for your health. Let me get you a glass of milk instead? It's time you take better care of yourself and the little one."

Audrey tucked the unlit cigarette back in her purse. "Sounds like excellent advice."

"It's none of my business, but you don't look the type who sleeps around."

"I'm not. Was I convincing? Don't want Frankie showing up when he gets out of prison to see his kid."

"I think you saw the last of Frankie, ma'am."

"Please, Phil. Call me Audrey."

"Do you need a ride home, Audrey?"

"Yes. Can you call a cab?"

"I'll do you one better. There's no reason to keep the cafe open. It's dead tonight. Suppose I close up early and give you a ride home?"

Audrey removed a near-full pack of Chesterfields from her purse and tossed it into the trash can. "I'd like that, Phil. I'd like that a lot."

Rainbow Bridge

My fear of death ended the day I left my remains on the highway pavement. To my surprise, I accepted and enjoyed an eternal afterlife, knowing I'd eventually reunite with my master. I was still a puppy when I met my fate, and I've waited seventy human years for Joey to meet his. It's been a long wait, but it'll be worth it when he claims me forever.

Not that I'm complaining. With vast meadows to play in and plenty of sunshine, what more could a dog ask for, aside from car rides, fire hydrants, and their humans? My furry friends' disabilities and illnesses no longer cripple them. Sick and old dogs become healthy pups again in this Shangri-La.

Joey was just eight years old when he picked me out of a litter of four. Because I'm a Dachshund, he named me Little Wienie. Give me a break. I'm a stud, not a stub. When we meet again, I'll discuss changing my name to a more respectable one for my breed, like Frank or Stretch.

Joey passed away last night. I'm at the lookout point where doggies wait to reunite with their masters before joining him on their final journey. I'm excited as a puppy to cross Rainbow Bridge into Heaven with my human, just like others before me. It's times like these I thank my lucky stars. I won't be one of those pets left stranded at the overpass to Heaven because their master never claimed them. A fate I wouldn't wish on a cat.

There he is. I'd know that scent anywhere. It's Joey. I wag my tail and run to him as fast as my short Dachshund legs can move. A Labrador Retriever gallops past me. Joey cries with happiness as he kneels to receive sloppy kisses from the oversized animal large enough to belong in the horse section. I catch up and nudge Joey's arm with my nose. I bark, *"I'm over here. It's Little Wienie."*

Joey reaches down and scratches behind my ears. "My goodness. You look the same as I remember you before you ran under the wheels of the truck seventy years ago. Good for you." He turns his attention to the dog with the name Thunder on his collar. "Sorry for the delay, boy. You've been so patient. We've been apart a long time, but you were never absent from my heart.

Once we cross to the other side, we'll be together forever."

I'm confused. Why talk to just Thunder instead of both of us? And what does he mean by "WE?"

Thunder and I follow Joey until we come to a sign. ONE PET BEYOND THIS POINT.

I cringe and feel sorry for Thunder, knowing he'll be Joey's second choice. He won't be going anywhere. It must suck to be him right now.

My tail swishes faster than a windshield wiper set at high speed when Joey picks me up and hugs me tight. He puts me on the ground again and kneels to look into the eyes of the oversized dog. This will be good. Here comes his farewell speech that will strike Thunder with a bolt of lightning.

"Thunder, we've been through so much together. You were my shadow during my adolescent and college days and at my side when I first kissed the woman who later became my wife. Not to mention the time you saved my son's life when you rescued him from drowning in the pool."

Thunder answers his human with more sloppy kisses.

I watch as Joey wipes a tear from his eye. "Putting you down was the hardest decision I ever made. But you were suffering. It was the humane thing to do. Now, look at you. I'm overjoyed we're together again and to see you so healthy."

I bark, *"Okay, Joey. The cat's out of the bag. One dog only. It's just you and me now."*

A hippy-looking guy with a beard, long hair, white robe, and sandals approaches us. "What's the delay over here?"

Joey points to the sign. "I never expected this. It's cruel to force someone to make such a tough decision."

"You're barking up the wrong tree, pal. I don't make the rules. Do you have any idea how crowded Heaven will get if pet owners bring all their animals with them? But after so many complaints, rumors are the higher-ups have discussed a policy to allow pet owners to choose more than one animal. Unfortunately, change takes time. We're talking eternity here. Give it another five hundred years, give or take a century or two. As head of bridge security, I have to enforce the current laws." He points toward

Thunder and me. "Make your choice. Select one. Move on."

Joey turns to me. "Sorry, Wienie. You read the sign. You were only in my life for eight months. We never got to know each other that well. The strict one animal policy forces me to leave you behind. I'm sure you understand."

"No, I don't understand," I growl as Joey and Thunder follow a rainbow and vanish into the distance.

This isn't fair. I came first. Thunder should wait in line. Why am I in the doghouse? I did nothing wrong. I never saw it coming. Joey gives me a humiliating name, makes me wait a human lifetime, and then rejects me as nothing more than a distant memory.

Then the animal shelter truck delivering its latest arrivals pulls into the welcoming headquarters parking lot. It reminded me of the time I came to this refuge. I knew nothing of this place and learned to adjust, but I never expected to be here forever.

How many of these new residents will reunite with their humans in the future? And who will go unclaimed like me? My despair and anger drive me to end it all. In a moment of déjà vu, I envision running under the wheels of the animal shelter truck. Then I think. Why?

Rainbow Bridge is paradise. It's not Heaven, but doggone close.

For now, I'll sniff around with my canine friends, chase balls, and learn new tricks. Until then, I'll wait until Joey returns to get me in another five hundred years. Give or take a century or two.

PURPLE HAZE

2014

Excuse me, Lou Gehrig, for borrowing your quote, but I consider myself the luckiest man on the face of the earth. I have fame, fortune, an incredible job, and our first baby is on its way.

My name is Tyler Fitzpatrick. Baseball fans know the deal. In 1995, the New York Yankees called me up to the majors, two years after a serious accident threatened to end my career. My last contract expires after this 2014 season. Time to hang up my spikes and concentrate on being a father. It will become a more rewarding experience than the walk-off home run I hit to win the World Series. Life is good, and it will only get better.

An off-day on the schedule allows me to drag my wife out of the office for lunch. Now, in her seventh month, I wish she'd work less.

As I approach Manhattan, fog with a purple tint rolls in. It reminds me of the Jimi Hendrix song, *Purple Haze*, even if the purple haze Hendrix sang about wasn't fog. My foot taps the brake pedal as I enter the mysterious cloud, but the car continues at high speed. I fight with the steering wheel as I swerve into the other lane, running an oncoming Cadillac off the road.

After regaining control, I pulled off to the shoulder of the highway and breathed a sigh of relief. Then the Cadillac I cut off earlier makes a U-turn and pulls behind me. The driver jumps from his car and approaches me at a quick pace. *Will I be a road-rage statistic?*

"Where'd you get your license?" he yells. "You damn near killed me."

"I'm so sorry, sir. As soon as I entered that purple haze, the car reacted as if no one was driving it."

"Purple haze? Are you hallucinating?" He removes a pen flashlight from his shirt pocket and shines it in my eyes. "I'm a doctor. Have you been drinking or taking substances that hinder your judgment?"

"Never. I'm Tyler Fitzpatrick."

"Should your name mean anything to me?"

"Guess you're not a baseball fan. You're talking to the shortstop for the New York Yankees."

"Derek Jeter was the shortstop the last time I looked at the lineup card."

"Who is Derek Jeter?"

"You must live in a cave if you don't know who Derek Jeter is." He checks my pulse. "I see nothing wrong, but I suggest a physical the first chance you get." He points at my forehead. "How'd you get that nasty scar?"

"I was visiting Manhattan's Financial District after Mr. Steinbrenner gave me a tour of Yankee Stadium. As I stood at a crowded intersection in front of the Stanford Exchange, a young girl crossed the street against the Don't Walk sign. A bus headed straight at her. I rushed into traffic and pushed her away just in time. But the bus knocked me headfirst onto the pavement, leaving me comatose for three days."

"You're lucky to be alive."

"You don't know how lucky. Without the accident, I wouldn't have met Gloria."

"Who's Gloria?"

"The kid I saved. I remained in touch with her and her father, investment magnate William H. Stanford.

The accident happened in front of his building. Twelve years later, she became my wife."

"A touching story, Mr. Fitzpatrick."

"It turned out that way. But it looked like my dream was over. Doctors said it was unlikely that I'd ever play ball again. Not even I expected to walk away from the game with a Hall of Fame career and a beautiful wife."

The doctor shook his head. "Derek Jeter will be a first-ballot Hall of Famer. Tyler Fitzpatrick? Don't think so."

I didn't bother bragging about my accomplishments on a baseball diamond to someone who had never heard of me. Despite his lack of sports knowledge, we shook hands, and I asked if he wanted my autograph. He looked at me as if I had two heads and said, "No, thank you."

I continue my drive to Manhattan. I slow down when I pass a billboard that always has my image. *Who is the good-looking guy with a dark complexion taking my space? Why is he wearing a Yankee uniform with my number 2?*

Because of my celebrity, it's been impossible to walk the city streets unnoticed. Yet today, autograph seekers aren't hounding me as I enter the Stanford Exchange building. I say hello to Janice, the receptionist, and continue toward the elevator.

She orders me to stop. "Hold on, sir. Nobody's allowed past the main lobby without security clearance."

"You can't be too careful these days, Janice, but why tell me?

"Whoever you are, you don't have that clearance."

"Whoever I am? You're kidding, right?"

"No, sir, I'm not. Who do you wish to see?"

"I have a lunch appointment with my wife."

"I'll call ahead and let her know you're here. You are?"

He sighed. "You know who I am. I'm Tyler Fitzpatrick."

"Fitzpatrick?" she mumbles as she scrolls through the employee list. "No one with that name works here."

"Gloria Stanford Fitzpatrick. The daughter of William H. Stanford. The CEO of the damn place. I can't believe you don't remember who I am."

"Please, sir, I'm not paid enough to deal with attitudes like yours."

"What attitude? You've seen me countless times in this building. Just last month, I gave your son an autographed baseball. Tyler Fitzpatrick doesn't need a security clearance. Excuse me. I know the way." I head toward the elevator.

The security guard I've seen working the building for years stops me. "Don't go any further. We don't want trouble here. Leave before I call the police."

"I'm Tyler Fitzpatrick."

"And I'm Elvis Presley. Get lost!"

"Gloria will vouch for me."

"Gloria, who?"

"Stanford. Gloria Stanford. My wife."

A minute later, the elevator door opens. Out steps my beautiful wife, looking as shapely as she did when we first married. "Front desk called me about a disturbance. What's going on?"

"Gloria? What happened to your belly?"

"Excuse me?"

"Our baby."

Gloria looks at Elvis for an explanation.

"This clown claims he's your husband, Ms. Stanford."

"The pervert should be so lucky. Remove the nut job from the building."

Elvis forces me outside, where a squad car just pulled in front of the building. A police officer asks, "Why are you stalking Ms. Stanford?"

"I'm not stalking anyone. I came for a lunch date with my wife. Why is she avoiding me? I'm her husband, Tyler Fitzpatrick. Everyone knows me."

"I don't," the officer answered. "Am I supposed to?"

"I'm the shortstop for the New York Yankees."

"Since when does Derek Jeter have blond hair?"

There's that name again. Who is this Jeter guy? When I woke up this morning, Tyler Fitzpatrick was a legend. Now, nobody knows who I am. I don't get it. I call out to the gathering crowd. "An autographed baseball for the first person who recognizes me. I'm Tyler Fitzpatrick, shortstop for the New York Yankees."

An elderly man wearing a Yankee cap answers, "Never heard of you. We already have a shortstop. Derek is doing a great job. Can you pitch?"

People have acted weird since I passed through that purple haze. I'm expecting my teammates to step from the shadows and say, "Smile! You're on Candid Camera."

The officer asks for my driver's license. I hand it to him.

"Mr. Fitzpatrick? This license expired years ago."

"Okay, I get it. My teammates are pulling a prank. It won't surprise me if Brett Gardner and C.C. are behind this."

The officer turns to his partner. "Cuff him while I call the station."

With my arms bound behind me, I stand on the crosswalk and watch a light fog with a purple tint roll in. Similar to the one I drove through this morning. Gloria and I make eye contact as she leaves the building and heads across the street for a waiting taxi. Halfway into the intersection, she turns to stare at me. "You look familiar. Have we met before?"

Before I answer, I see a speeding bus heading in her direction. With no time to warn her, I dart from the walkway and give her a shoulder block, pushing her from the bus's path. The squeal of brakes and a loud thud are the last sounds I hear.

Only a set of locked handcuffs lay on the street.

"Where did he go, officer?" Gloria asks. "I saw him vanish right in front of my eyes. It was like puff, and he was gone."

"I witnessed it too, Ms. Stanford. The computer database matched the license to a guy who died in a bus accident back in 1993. The freaky part is the accident happened at this intersection."

"Oh, my God! A name, officer? I need a name?"

"Tyler Fitzpatrick, ma'am. Does the name ring a bell?"

LEAVING WORK EARLY

"This sucks," Robin complained. "Friday is the busiest day of the week, and Mrs. O'Neil cuts out before lunch."

"Tell me about it," Sandy grunted as she bit into her tuna sandwich. "If we did that crap, she would be all over us. You'd think as our supervisor, she'd be more responsible."

"It's not fair. Mrs. O'Neil has been doing this for a month, leaving us to work our assess off and cover for her."

"What's even less fair is how she got the promotion. We're just as qualified as she is."

"It's all about appearance, Sandy. We both know the game and how she became our boss. Women with her looks can open doors you and I can't. We don't stand a chance in the corporate world. I'm an overweight Afro-American, and you may be a blonde like Mrs. O'Neil, but no offense, similarities end there. Ever wonder who her boyfriend is?"

"She has a boyfriend?"

"Open your eyes. Friday is dress-down day. While we come to work wearing jeans and T-shirts, she struts in here all dolled up with low-cut blouses and high heels. It's obvious why she leaves early. She's seeing someone."

"Your imagination is running away with you, Robin. She's married."

"Most likely so is her lover. Why else would she split at noontime? While their spouses are working, Mrs. O'Neil and her stud take Friday afternoons off for fun and games."

A smile came across Sandy's face. "You know what? Mrs. O'Neil won't return to the office today. Why don't we split too? There's no way she'd find out."

"Good idea. It'll give me a chance to buy my husband's birthday present without him looking over my shoulder."

"And I can catch up with my gardening before the kids come home from school."

"What if she finds out? What then?"

"How would she know? Let's do it, Robin."

That night, Sandy called Robin. "Forget doing that shit again. I almost got caught."

"How on earth did that happen?"

"Would you believe it? I walked upstairs to change into my gardening clothes, and I found Mrs. O'Neil naked in bed with my husband. Damn! I had to sneak out of the house before she saw me. If she found out I left work early, she'd fire me for sure."

I Sold My Soul to the Devil
With Daniel Charles McCarthy

"This is bullshit," I argued after my agent read me the riot act. "The editing changes you suggest are unnecessary. This is a future bestseller, yet you tell me you can't get my novel published. What's wrong with this picture? So much for your connections with the top publishers in the field."

"Publishing companies hesitate to sign new authors. You have the talent and imagination. What you don't have is a marketable story." She handed me a list of negative comments. "Tweak and resubmit. I'll take another look."

I skimmed the suggestions, disagreeing with most. Killing off the main character in the last chapter was not happening. "It's my story, dammit. He's needed for the sequel."

"A sequel? You can't even get the book published, and you're talking sequel?" She stood from her desk. "If you refuse to take my suggestions, we're wasting each other's time. I work on commission. Fifteen percent of nothing won't pay my bills." She pointed to the door. "Do me a favor. Find another agent."

I stormed from her office, shouting, "I'd sell my soul to the devil for a publishing contract, but I won't rewrite my novel."

The elevator door opened. Inside stood a strange-looking dude, wearing a cape and carrying a pitchfork. I was about to ask if he was attending a costume party when he introduced himself as Satan.

"Did I hear you offer to sell your soul to the devil for a publishing contract?"

"It was a figure of speech, pal. I didn't mean it literally."

"Too bad. Because I can guarantee your book becomes a bestseller, as will all your future work."

"How can you make that promise?"

His piercing red eyes gazed at me. "I'm the devil. I can do what the hell I please."

"What's the catch?"

"The service is free, for now. Over the next three years, your books will sell millions of copies, your name mentioned in the same breath as the masters. From the publication date of your first book, the clock ticks. On the third anniversary, your soul will belong to me." He removed a document from his cape. "Sign here."

After reading the contract, I questioned the fine print. "If you want my John Hancock, make one change. I have a wife and kid at home. The success you promise is tempting, but I must protect my interests. Add an escape clause. If you don't take my soul on the anniversary date, our contract becomes invalid."

Two horns grew from his forehead. "The devil doesn't modify, nor does he forget dates. But, if it makes you more comfortable, I'll add the ridiculous escape clause. It won't make a hell of a difference."

Hell & Back Press called the following day, offering me a publishing contract where I wouldn't be making any revisions, which I was unhappy with. Within three months, my book flew off the shelves at Barnes & Noble. Amazon sales broke records. Soon after, it appeared on every best-seller list. Two successful follow-up sequels bypassed sales of J. K. Rowling's Harry Potter series.

On my novel's third anniversary, I booked a cruise to New Zealand. If Satan came to collect on the contract and take my soul, he had a surprise coming. I had other plans. Satan might not forget dates, but did he know geography?

My wife slept in the cabin while I enjoyed the fresh cool air on the balcony. Satan joined me a minute past midnight. He flashed a devilish grin. "Happy Anniversary."

"We are in the middle of the ocean. How did you get on board?"

"I'm the devil. I'm anywhere. Did you think you could hide from me? It's time to collect your soul."

"Not just yet. Before we complete the deal, follow me to the captain's quarters. It concerns the escape clause."

"Stop stalling. You signed the contract. You have no escape."

"We'll see about that."

After finding the captain, I asked, "Is it true we just passed over the International Date Line?"

The captain nodded. "I'm adjusting the ship's log to reflect the twenty-four-hour gain as we speak. Five minutes ago, the calendar said November 15. At midnight, it became November 17. We skipped a day when we crossed over it."

Satan's pupils turned from red to black. "What the hell is the International Date Line?"

"It's the imaginary line separating two calendar days," the captain explained. "A traveler heading eastbound subtracts a day, while westbound travelers add a day."

The devil asked, "What does this mean?"

"I hate to tell you this, Satan. You've been outdated. The added escape clause says you must collect my soul on this November 16th. You're a day late. I'm free from any contractual commitments."

Satan's horns vibrated. He cursed the lord. In an uncontrollable rage, he leaped over the railing into the cold, dark waters of the Pacific Ocean, sending up a geyser of steam.

The captain reached for a life preserver.

"Don't bother," I said. "He's the devil. Let him go to hell."

PILLOW TALK

"What happened?" I groaned, realizing I was in a hospital bed with a cast on each arm. My head hurt like hell. My wife stood over me.

"You were in a car accident. A tractor-trailer rear-ended you. You've been in a coma since Sunday."

"Damn. Anyone else hurt?"

"A woman died at the scene, but it wasn't your fault. She shouldn't have been where she was."

"I feel terrible."

"So do I, John. but in your condition, you have more urgent matters to worry about."

"I need to know. How old was the woman? Did she have any children?"

"She was my age, and like us, had a daughter in college."

The nurse entered the room. "Oh, my gosh, Mr. Peterson. You're awake. How are you feeling?"

"My head is pounding. It hurts to breathe. My body aches all over."

"You have three cracked ribs, a separated right shoulder, and a broken left collarbone. Not to mention you were comatose for three days. You're fortunate to be alive."

"So, I heard. Mary Catherine was explaining the accident, my injuries, and the woman that died when you walked into the room."

"Mary Catherine?"

"My wife." I turned my head to the left to introduce her to the nurse. She wasn't there. "That strange? She was at my bedside when you walked in. Where did she go?"

"Mr. Peterson? I saw nobody aside from you when I entered the room. Besides, it's two a.m. Visiting hours are long over. You were most likely dreaming."

"This was no dream. Mary Catherine was here. Didn't you see her when you walked in?"

"No, I didn't."

"I don't get. Why would she hide?"

"Maybe because it's past visiting hours, and she doesn't want to get in trouble."

"Mary Catherine. Come out from wherever you are."

After no reply, the nurse looked under the beds and in the patient's bathroom. "Nope, she's not here. I'll check the cafeteria."

When the doctor on call arrived, he poked around, checked my reflexes, and shined a flashlight in my eyes before he read my charts. "His vitals are good, Nurse Siegal. Watch him closely until Doctor Jacobs makes his rounds in the morning."

The nurse followed the doctor into the hallway. "Doctor, I need to bring this to your attention. Our patient is alert but insists he was talking to his wife earlier."

"It's not uncommon. Medication contributes to hallucinations. Give the patient time. Mr. Peterson has gone through hell."

The hours went by. It was now ten o'clock. Visiting hours had just begun when Mary Catherine returned to the room. "Sorry for disappearing, John. I shouldn't be here."

"What the hell happened? Last I remember, I was on my way to the office to work on the company's new website with Jackie Grant."

"You mean Jaclyn. Why didn't you tell me Jackie was a female?"

"I didn't want you to get the wrong idea."

"Why? Just because she has long, shapely legs, a tight butt, and boobs larger than bowling balls doesn't make her a threat."

"Aren't you exaggerating?"

"Am I? She's been flaunting everything she owns during her visits to your bedside. For Christ's sake, this is a hospital, not an Academy Awards dinner."

"What are you saying?"

"I'm not stupid. Website my ass."

Just then, Jackie rushed to my bedside, dressed to kill.

My heart skipped a beat, knowing my wife was in the room. I turned toward Mary Catherine to see her reaction, but she was not there. *Where did she go? She was standing in front of me ten seconds earlier.*

"Thank God you're okay, honey. You had me worried. My world is empty without you."

"Hush, Jackie," I whispered. "My wife is on to us. Keep your voice down. She's in the room somewhere."

"Your wife?"

I nodded and called out, "Mary Catherine. Where are you? This is the second time you've disappeared." When she didn't answer, I told Jackie to look everywhere.

"She's not here. Trust me."

"I'm telling you, Jackie. I was speaking to her seconds before you entered the room. Please, just look!"

Jackie looked in the same spots as Nurse Siegal did and the same thing. She wasn't in the room. "Nope, she's not here. You must have been dreaming."

"I was awake. I swear! Mary Catherine was here. She suspects something is going on between us."

"Why should you care? You promised to divorce her anyway, right?"

"Yeah, but still, let's back off for a while." He looked up and saw Mary Catherine standing in the doorway, her arms folded across her chest. "Shit! She's watching us. Watch what you say. She might hear you."

"Who?"

"Mary Catherine. She's looking right at us."

"Trust me, big boy. She's not here."

Nurse Siegal walked in. "Good morning, Ms. Grant. How's our patient doing?"

"Can we talk in private?" Jackie whispered. The two women walked into the hall. "John is acting weird. He's delusional. Thinks he saw his wife standing in the doorway."

"Don't worry too much, Mrs. Grant. He was behaving the same way last night when he first woke up. I brought it to the doctor's attention. It's a temporary condition. But it might be best if we cut his visiting hours short today."

"When should we tell him? He needs to know the truth."

"Doctor Jacobs wishes to wait. Mr. Peterson needs time before he learns the sad news."

As Jackie and Nurse Siegel spoke in the corridor, Mary Catherine reappeared at her husband's bedside. "They're talking about us, John."

"Where were you hiding?"

"If anyone should hide, it's you."

"Who should I hide from?"

"Me. You hired Jackie to help with the company website over the weekends. You needed her expertise until the site was up and running. It's been two months. What's the delay?"

"Websites are tricky. We still have glitches to work out. It's coming. We'll get it."

"I'm sure it's been cumming, and the both of you have already gotten it."

"What are you talking about?"

"Why didn't you pick up when I called your office two Sundays ago?"

"I didn't hear the phone ring."

"That's because you weren't in the office."

"Where would I be?"

"You tell me."

"You should have called my cell."

"I did. You were too busy to answer."

"I'm never too busy to speak to you, my dear?"

"If I believe that, I must also believe in the tooth fairy."

"Why not mention it when I got home?"

"Because you answered my question without saying a word."

"How'd I do that?"

"The scent of a perfume that I don't use, but Jackie does."

"What do you expect? Jackie and I are working our tails off on the website. We were working in close quarters."

"Real close."

"There you go again. I told you nothing is going on between us. Will you stop being so suspicious?"

"How can I not be? Especially after I researched your website partner. She's a receptionist working for one of your clients. She knows less about computers than I do. According to her boss, she took a leave of absence because of a personal matter. I put the pieces together. Even Stevie Wonder could see what's going on."

"You got the wrong idea. Jackie and I would never cross over the line."

"Spare me, John. The day of your accident, I hid in your trunk to take pictures of wherever you go with Jackie for the divorce lawyer. Unfortunately, I never used the camera because the tractor-trailer plowed into you when you slowed down to enter the parking lot of the Waterfront Motel."

"If you were in my trunk, why weren't you injured? You look fine to me."

"Not as fine as Jackie, I assume. Let me put it this way. I felt no pain."

"What are you saying?"

"I'm dead, John. But before I'm gone for good, I have a score to settle."

I broke out in laughter and coughed. "It hurts to laugh, but worth it to hear my deadpan wife's comic side. What's the occasion?"

"Isn't laughter the best medicine, my dear?"

"It sure is, but please, save your one-liners until my ribs heal so I can appreciate your humor."

"I'm here for a reason. It's not to tell jokes. I just wonder how police will figure out what happened?" She slid the other bed against the door, wedging it shut.

"What's about to happen, Mary Catherine?"

"This!" She removed a pillow from the vacant bed and held it over my face. I fought for my life, but with my arms in casts, she overpowered me. The last words I heard were, "Sweet dreams, John."

YOUNG AT HEART

The family tradition every Christmas was to visit our grandparents and sit around the fireplace toasting marshmallows. Mom and Grandma were cooking supper in the kitchen while Gramps rambled on about how he and his friends built a snowman that came to life. With his arms waving in the air and his complexion turning as red as the few strands of hair left on his head, his animated gestures added to an already fascinating tale.

My attention locked in on Gramp's every word as he described how he, little Joey, and Mikey did all the work while Sally supervised. As the story goes, apart from sticking a corncob pipe in the snowman's mouth, Sally did nothing but boss everyone around. It was when Joey placed an old silk hat on the snowman's head the miracle happened.

The details of Gramps' story were as vivid as turning the pages of a picture book that magically came alive. Oh, how I wished I had been there.

On our drive home, I raved about how cool it must have been to play with a living snowman.

Mom mumbled, "God! Here we go again. The snowman story. When will this ever end?"

"He's harmless, dear," Daddy said. "You should be used to it by now."

"He's your father. Is this how you'll be when you reach his age? For God's sake, he believes his snowman came to life. What kind of message is he sending to little Tommy?"

"Let it be, honey. Like I said, it's harmless."

Mom turned to me in the backseat. "Your grandfather told an amazing story, but it's not real."

"Gramps wouldn't lie. He wouldn't."

My father chimed in with a few words. "Grandpa is in la-la land. We enjoy his tales, but sometimes he exaggerates."

"Where's la-la-land, Daddy?"

"It's a place your mind goes when it crosses the line between reality and fantasy. Gramps has been insisting his snowman came to life for so long now, he won't admit he made it up."

"Are you sure, Daddy? Gramps said he and his friends will meet the snowman again someday."

"Your grandfather hasn't seen or heard from his friends since he was a kid not much older than you. And c'mon, son. You're seven years old. Old enough to know a snowman can't come to life."

***

As I grew older, I realized my grandfather's snowman tale was just that... a tale. A very tall one. But his aging mind believed it was real, and he hung on to the notion his friends would return to help build a snowman that would come to life and play just the same as you and me.

When my parents retired to Florida fifteen years ago, Gramps refused to join them because it didn't snow down South. I wondered if this was an excuse so he wouldn't have to leave the only neighborhood he ever lived in or if Gramps was that obsessed with his fantasy.

Rather than turn his world upside down, my wife and I honored his wishes. We moved our growing family into his larger house and looked after him. He kept to himself most of the time, except during the Christmas holidays. It was then when he'd retell his snowman story to my children. If he lived long enough, he'd do the same to my grandkids. It amazed me how he kept the details as consistent as I remember hearing them when I was a kid.

When meteorologists predicted the biggest snowstorm in decades, Gramps turned up the television, listening to the forecast. I saw the grin on his face as he stared out the window with his winter gear at his side as he counted every snowflake.

Not knowing where his thoughts were, I tested his grip on reality. "It looks like you're about to explore the North Pole, Gramps. What's going on?"

"They'll be here soon, Tommy."

"Who?"

"Little Joey, Mikey, and Sally. This is our last chance. We're not getting any younger, you know."

"Your friends are not coming in this weather. Besides, you haven't seen or heard from them in ages."

"They'll show. I'm sure of it. When we were kids, he promised to be back again someday. We pinky swore to be here for him. It's been eighty years. How would it look if we didn't show?"

"The snowman won't return, Gramps. He melted a long time ago. And you'd be foolish to think after eighty years that your friends would show up at the door ready for a reunion with a glob of snow. Be real. Stop living in a dream world."

"I'm not a fool. You sound just like your father. He thought I made it up. It happened just the way I said, yet nobody ever believed me. Why?"

"You can't go out in this nasty weather."

"Don't tell me what to do, Tommy. I'm old enough to make my own decisions."

The doorbell rang, interrupting our argument. Gramps limped to the door, saying, "It's for me."

An old lady, supporting herself with a cane and holding a corncob pipe, stood on the stoop.

"Sally. It's been a long time. I was expecting you."

"Hurry, Red. The gang is waiting. We got work to do. Move it."

"I'll be out in a minute."

Gramps disappeared into his room. I told the old woman my grandfather wasn't going out in this storm.

"He better come. We're counting on him." She turned and headed off the stoop. When she reached the platform, she said, "Sorry for being rude, sonny boy, but I ain't got time to be sociable. Gotta supervise."

Sally hobbled toward the side of the house, where two elderly men struggled to roll a small snowball into a large one. One man sat in a wheelchair, while the other depended on a walker.

Gramps stepped out of his room dressed in a heavy winter coat, boots, mittens, and ski cap, all set to join his friends.

I blocked his path. "Where do you think you're going?"

"Don't stand in my way. I've been waiting for this reunion for a long time. I'm going out there to help. You're not stopping me."

"You're not leaving the house."

"For God's sake. Listen to Sally. She sounds like a drill sergeant out there. Mikey and Joey need help. It won't be easy building a snowman at our ages."

"Get this through your thick skull, Gramps. It's twenty degrees outside. You are ninety years old. Do you want to risk getting pneumonia or falling and breaking your neck?"

"My friends are the same age as me and have no problem going out there. Chill out! I'm dressed for the occasion."

I grabbed his arm to stop him as he walked toward the front door. Determined, thick-headed Gramps would not take no for an answer.

Against my better judgment, I stepped aside and allowed him to join his friends. I followed behind.

"Stay out of our way, sonny boy. We got this," Sally warned as I watched the four senior citizens build their snowman with precision engineering. I offered to help. Sally shooed me away. "You have nothing to do with this."

After the four finished their creation, the crusty old lady shoved a corncob pipe in the snowman's mouth. All eyes focused on Joey as he removed an old silk hat from a compartment of his wheelchair. His disability wouldn't allow him to stand and reach the snowman's head, so Sally took the hat and handed it to Gramps. "You were always the tallest, Red. You know what to do."

"I sure do, Sally. My grandson is even taller. He should get the honors." He handed the hat to me. "You heard my snowman story a dozen times. I know you don't believe it's true, but you soon will. So, I'm leaving it to you to pass on the legacy."

"Face reality, guys. There is no guarantee this hat will still have its magic after all these years."

"We got no time for speeches," Sally grumbled as she cut me off. "Let's get the show on the road, sonny boy. Put the hat on his head already. We got lots to do before he melts away."

Foreseeing the glob of snow was not coming to life, I prepared them for the worst. "This is an old hat, guys. When things get old, they sometimes don't work like they used to. The magic the hat once had may no longer be there."

"Don't be so damn negative. My friends and I are also old. Age is only a number. We may not be as agile as we once were, but we're not dead. Look at the detail of the snowman we just constructed. He's a masterpiece. Michelangelo couldn't have done a better job. This is our creation, and we are proud of the finished product. We did our part, so don't tell me the old hat will let us down." Sally rested her hands on her hips. "If you can't do a simple task, I'll get a ladder and do it myself."

"Sally," I argued. "Climbing a ladder at your age is near suicide."

"You know nothing about me. I was an athletic tomboy in my day and climbed trees taller than a house. I may not move around as fast as I once did, but I can get it done if I put my mind to it. So don't tell me what I can and cannot do." She pointed to the shed. "Is that where you keep the ladder?"

"You're not a kid anymore. Didn't I tell you climbing a ladder at your age is dangerous?"

"You're no spring chicken yourself. And I'm the youngest of the clan. I won't turn eighty-nine until the summer."

"Alright, Sally. No need for a ladder. I can easily reach the snowman's head."

"What are you waiting for? We don't have all day. Put the hat on his head already."

After I followed Sally's orders, I stepped back. The senior citizens waited for a miracle that would not happen.

Sally pointed toward the house. "How about some privacy? Go fix yourself a cup of hot chocolate or something. Do you get my drift? Take a hike. Don't screw this up for us."

Bossy Sally had a way with words. Rather than lecture her on etiquette, I went inside, not wanting to witness their disappointment. After not hearing the noisy chatter from the senior citizens for a while, I peeked out the window to make sure everything was okay. It wasn't. Gramps and his friends had disappeared. Left behind was an empty wheelchair, an overturned walker, and a discarded cane. The snowman was nowhere in sight.

I ran from the house and followed a trail of footprints that ended on a street corner. I asked the traffic cop if he saw four senior citizens and a snowman come this way.

"The strangest sight I ever saw," he answered. "I hollered stop, but they only paused for a moment." He pointed toward the hilly field across the street. "They went in that direction."

I trudged through the snow over the hills until I found a group of young children struggling to upright their fallen snowman. I stopped to help lift it back on its base and asked, "I'm looking for four old people. By any chance, did you see them?"

"No sir," answered the redheaded boy before asking the girl next to him. "How about you, Sally?"

"You're only as old as you feel, mister. If any old people are out in this storm, they must be young at heart and feeling frisky." She winked at her other two friends. "Joey? Mikey? Did you see any 'old people' come by?"

NAUGHTY NANCY

Nancy Holliday got the cold shoulder from her boss, Brad Sanford when they crossed each other's path in the cafeteria before working hours began. Other than a simple head nod, he avoided her as he thumbed through the sports pages of the morning newspaper.

"Why treat me like a stranger, Brad?" she asked. "What's wrong?"

"We'll talk later, Nance." His eyes rolled as J.T. approached them.

"Mrs. Holliday," J.T. said in a stern voice. "My father expects you in the conference room at nine-thirty. Be there." He turned to Brad. "My office."

Brad tossed the newspaper on the counter, gulped the rest of his coffee, and followed J.T. to the elevator.

This is turning into a strange day, Nancy thought. *Why did Brad brush me off? What's with the formality of J.T. calling me Mrs. Holliday? Now the company president wants to meet with me. Whatever is going on, I don't like it.*

Punctual as always, Nancy arrived five minutes early. Old man Worthington sat in his usual place at the head of the table.

"Close the door," he ordered in a somber tone as he pointed to a chair alongside him.

Nancy's heart raced.

Worthington spoke. "Five years ago, because of Lora Cane's recommendation, Genesis hired you as a temporary replacement in sales. Your intelligence and ability to learn on the fly impressed us enough to give you a permanent position in the marketing department. It didn't take long to make a name for yourself. I never regretted my decision to appoint you as our department manager."

"I love my job, but I feel terrible my promotion caused a conflict with Lora. Brad promised her the position when it became available. I feel like I betrayed her."

"You didn't ask for the job. Brad, your strongest supporter, thought you had better qualifications, despite Lora's marketing and accounting degrees."

"Still, she resents me. We'd been best friends since grammar school. Now we don't speak anymore unless it's work-related."

"Don't worry about Lora. After she lost out on the promotion, she asked for a transfer to accounting. It didn't take long to work her way up the ladder to become the company comptroller. Her salary might not be as high as yours, but she does okay." Worthington's fingers twirled the remote control for the monitor hanging on the wall. "Although there has been no official announcement, I'm sure you've heard of my forced retirement."

Nancy didn't know how to respond. Brad leaked the confidential news to her a month ago. Only a handful of people knew. I'm not supposed to be one of them. "It's the first I heard of this, sir."

"My next birthday is my seventieth. The Board of Directors will put me out to pasture by year's end. They forget how my leadership saved Genesis from bankruptcy twelve years ago."

Nancy chose her words carefully. "The Worthington legacy will last forever. The stockholders appreciate what you've done for them."

"If that's the case, why treat me like a dinosaur?"

"Mr. Worthington. Your job is stressful, especially with the economy the way it is. Don't forget your mild heart attack last year. You don't need any undue pressure that could compromise your health. It's time, Mr. Worthington. It makes sense to bring in younger blood with new ideas."

"J.T. is waiting in the wings. Why is the board bypassing my son as my successor?"

The old man put Nancy on the spot. Everyone in the company knew J.T. was useless. If he hadn't been the boss's son, he wouldn't be vice president.

When she didn't answer, Worthington cuffed his hand over his ear. "I don't hear you, Nancy. I asked you a question. Answer it!"

"I can't answer that, sir."

"You can't, or you won't?"

Nancy's knee-jerking shook the table. "Nothing against J.T., sir, but Brad has ideas to improve profits."

"The economic downslide is hurting everyone. Genesis is not the only corporation going through rough times. With my son's leadership, profits will bounce back."

"Payroll costs have increased since we've added outside sales reps. Brad believes these additions are counterproductive and are not helping sales. He's pushing for an outside audit to find out where to cut costs."

Worthington shifted in his chair. "How do you know so much about Brad's plans?"

"I work under him. We talk a lot."

He leaned back in his chair and rolled his eyes. "Working under him is an understatement, although not much business talk goes on during those intimate moments." Worthington clicked the remote play button. "Watch the video. It's self-explanatory."

A lump formed in Nancy's throat when she recognized the Lakeside Motel parking lot. The camera focused on her green Infinity. She mumbled under her breath, "Shit." The Mercedes parked in the space next to her had a vanity license plate that read *MR. BS*. The car belonged to Brad Sanford. Worthington gave her a stern look.

"I don't know what to say, sir."

The video continued to run. The timestamp in the lower corner said it was two a.m. Nancy and Brad walked out of room #107, with Brad's hand tucked inside her cardigan. Worthington clicked the pause button and swiveled in his chair to face Nancy. "Do you have anything to say?"

"I made a mistake just that one time."

"I see, and I suppose nothing went on while you two worked all night when hackers broke into our website last week?"

"Mr. Worthington! Please. We worked our rear ends off until we resolved the problem. I swear, nothing happened. It was all work and no play."

Worthington fast-forwarded to a scene in Brad's office. "If this is nothing, I'd like to see how wild and crazy it gets when something is happening. You and Brad have set a new standard for the meaning of working overtime."

Nancy's hand covered her mouth at the sight of her naked self as she performed like a porno queen.

"*Shit!* Turn it off. I've seen enough. I'm so embarrassed."

"Ashamed is a more accurate term. Brad has a wife and three small children. A wife who is my daughter. What you have done is inexcusable."

"I'm sorry, Mr. Worthington."

"An apology doesn't erase your sins, nor does it explain to my grandchildren why Daddy won't be living at home anymore." He slammed his fist on the table and raised his voice. "How long have you two been intimate?"

Nancy dropped her head and whispered in a timid voice, "A while, sir."

"Be more specific."

"Around the time Brad campaigned for my promotion."

Worthington sighed. "You're an extraordinary talent, but my employees can't go around screwing one another."

"I've only been intimate with Brad."

"I don't give a damn if you're taking on half the men in the company, or as you say, 'only Brad.' It doesn't make a hell of a difference." He reached over to tap Nancy's wedding ring. "Brad is a great salesperson. He gave you a line of bullshit to get you in bed. You bought it. A married woman shouldn't have been a shopper."

She bowed her head. She committed adultery with the boss's son-in-law.

He placed the DVD into the protective case and tucked it inside his suit jacket pocket. "I've called for an emergency board meeting tomorrow to announce the dismissal of two of the company's most influential employees."

"We're fired?"

"The nation's largest distributor of bibles and religious artifacts can't have their employees display such behavior."

"Our affair hasn't interfered with work."

"We can't risk word leaking to our competitors. I expect resistance from the board when they learn of yours and Brad's termination." The old man flashed a smile. "Once they view this video, they'll applaud my decision."

"Please, don't do this. Pete Dickinson is on the board. He and my husband belong to the same country club. With his big mouth, the word is certain to get back to Steve."

"You should have thought of the consequences before you gave yourself to a married man. Don't expect any sympathy from me. You made your bed, Nancy. Now you can sleep in it with Brad anytime you want." He pointed to the door. "Clean out your office. Leave the building before coworkers ask questions."

Nancy fought back the tears as she left the conference room, avoiding eye contact when she saw Lora in the lobby.

***

Worthington waved a DVD in the air when Lora entered the room. "All the proof we need. Thanks to my private detective and Brad's cheating dick, no one will look any further into the finances at Genesis."

"Why did Nancy leave the conference room in tears?"

"It's not your problem. What's important is we have enough dirt to bury Brad. He's history once he broke the morality clause in his contract. We nailed him big time." Worthington motioned Lora to take a seat as he placed the DVD into the machine.

The video showed a naked woman performing oral sex with Brad. Her face was unrecognizable until she came up for air. "Shit!" Lora shrieked. "It's Nancy! I don't want to see this."

"Watch it, so you'll know why your once best friend got the promotion. Brad was right. Nancy had better qualifications than you."

When view time ended, he slid the laptop across the table and handed Lora the master and an unopened package of DVDs. "You're the computer whiz. Make backups."

"How many?"

"The entire pack."

"Mr. Worthington. I understand a copy or two, but twenty-five?"

"Freebees to pass around the office. I'll give one to my daughter's divorce attorney, FedEx, another to her husband."

"Nancy was my best friend. Sending one to Steve or handing out copies like trade magazines is going to extremes."

"Your problem, Lora, is your lack of a killer instinct."

"Our target is Brad. Leave Nancy out of this. If you intend to stoop so low, I want no part of it."

"Where is your loyalty?"

"This has gotten out of control. I want out."

"Your only out is prison. So, make the damn copies or explain why you signed over a half-million dollars of forged checks in the past two years."

With the threat of prison hanging over her head, Lora made backup after backup. While she did this, old man Worthington sat feet from her on the phone with J.T. Junior. She overheard him tell his son to drop by his office after finishing his conference call with

Cardinal Pulaski and Bishop McKenzie. He had a video he'll enjoy watching.

After completing her task, she handed the burned copies and the original to her boss. "Anything else, Mr. Worthington?"

"Yeah. Since Brad isn't here to look over our shoulder anymore, add another employee to the payroll."

"Mr. Worthington! The company is struggling financially. Now's not the time to get greedy. We should lie low for a while."

"Lora? I'm the boss here. I have the authority to hire whoever I please. Now shut up and get it done."

"I'll get right on it, sir." Lora walked to the door and turned, "Mr. Worthington? If you don't mind, can I scoot out for a few minutes? I need to pick up something at home?"

"Can't it wait until lunchtime?"

"No, it can't."

"Make it quick, Lora. Hurry back."

Lora replied, "This won't take long."

***

Nancy hung the *Do Not Disturb* sign outside her office door and locked herself inside. She paced the floor, talking to herself. "How will I explain getting fired to my husband?"

When someone knocked on the door. Nancy yelled, "Get lost. Can't you read the damn sign?"

"It's Lora. We need to talk."

"I'm not in the mood for chit-chat."

Lora jiggled the doorknob. "Unlock the door. I came to help."

"You're the last person I'd expect to show your face around here. Besides, nobody can help. Leave me alone."

"Nancy, hear me out."

"Shit!" Nancy grunted as she opened the door to let her in before she locked it again. "You have one minute to grab my attention before I throw you out the same window I'm about to jump out of. Start talking." The countdown began. "59 seconds... 58... 57..."

"Nancy, there's a conspiracy to dump Brad. He's a threat to Worthington's empire. The old man doesn't want him snooping around."

The countdown stopped. "What's going on? Is Worthington hiding something?"

"I'm getting to that. As much of a womanizer as Brad is, he cared about the company. With him insisting on an audit, Worthington needs to stop him."

"Brad carried Genesis for years," Nancy said, "yet the old man received the credit. With Brad gone and J.T. in charge, the company will have more financial issues than ever."

"The bastards care only about themselves. They'll do whatever is necessary to protect their own interests. Son-in-law or not, Mr. Worthington wants Brad gone, even at his daughter's expense."

"What you're saying sounds interesting, but Brad and I are no longer employees at Genesis." She pointed toward the door. "Time's up. Leave."

"Nancy. I saw the video."

"What! Why did Worthington play it to you?"

"I'm involved with something way over my head. It needs to stop now." She handed her a notebook and ledger. "It's all documented in here. But don't worry. I erased the master sex tape when computer idiot Worthington ordered me to make copies."

Nancy reached for a Kleenex to wipe tears from her eyes. "Lora, who do I thank first? You or God?"

"Just promise you'll give this information to the proper authorities."

"What have you gotten into?"

"When Frank Levy announced he'd retire at year's end, Brad approached me about becoming Levy's replacement as the next marketing manager. As you know, a huge pay raise came with the job. But there was a catch. All I had to do was ..." She gave Nancy a nervous laugh. "Then you entered the competition. You must be better in bed."

Nancy embraced her once good friend. "I'm so sorry."

"It's not your fault. I shouldn't have bought that Corvette and townhouse before my promotion became official. When I didn't get the job, I fell behind on my bills and got desperate."

"Desperate? As in?"

"I added a fictitious outside salesperson to the payroll. She got a check every week, which I cashed. Fifty thousand dollars later, J.T. caught wind of my scheme. He threatened to call the police unless I included him and the old man in the action. We were to split the earnings three ways. We soon added another employee and another to the payroll."

The loud banging on the door startled Nancy. "Open up," ordered J.T. "We know Lora is in there."

"Oops!" Lora said. "Looks like they didn't like what they didn't see when they played back the DVD."

Old man Worthington was more vocal. "Wait till I get my hands on you, you cocksucker."

Lora removed a pistol from her pocketbook.

Nancy gasped. "What are you doing with a gun?"

Before she answered, the Worthington's broke through the door and charged at Lora. She raised her pistol. Her first shot felled the old man in his tracks. J.T. was the target of her following two bullets. Two dead men lay at her feet.

Her hand trembled as she gazed at her two bosses with a blank stare in her eyes. "The old man said I lacked the killer instinct. How wrong he was. This gun holds six bullets. I have one remaining."

"I counted three shots. What happened to the other two bullets?"

"I used them to say goodbye to Brad in the parking lot." Lora aimed the gun at her head. "The remaining bullet has my name on it."

"Lora, don't!" Nancy cried out.

One final gunshot ended Lora's journey. Nancy gasped as her friend collapsed to the floor in a pool of blood.

NOT JUST A GAME

1962

My heart pounded as I stepped into the batter's box, dragging my bat behind. With two outs in the last inning, down by a run, I needed to reach base. Waiting in the on-deck circle stood all-star Lenny Perkins, the league's best hitter. Cheers from the dugout meant to encourage only increased my anxiety. At fourteen years old, I had already given up. Looking for a walk, my hopes changed after Johnny Valeo's blazing fastball split the middle of home plate.

"Swing the bat, in case you hit it," Perkins yelled as he blasted me with malicious rants on how terrible I was.

I wanted to disappear. Knees wobbling, I waited for another fastball. My bat crossed the plate long after the ball landed in the catcher's mitt.

The umpire raised his right hand. "Strike two!"

My team needed me to get on base and keep the inning alive. The moans coming from the dugout signaled my teammates had given up on me. I looked forward to what was coming next, as much as a visit to the dentist. I squeezed the bat handle. Tears clouded my eyes. Perkins continued his insults. "You stink. My kid sister hits better than you. If we lose this game, it'll be your fault."

"Time out," Valeo called. He motioned for his catcher to join him on the mound. The battery mates gathered. They gazed at the on-deck circle, listening to Perkins' painful criticism of my lack of athletic ability.

After allowing them enough time to discuss their strategy, the umpire broke up the meeting. Play resumed. The catcher crouched behind home plate. "Don't let big mouth on deck bother you. Perkins ain't as good as he thinks."

I feared the next pitch, a fastball I wouldn't see, would be the game's last. Instead, Valeo surprised me when he lobbed the ball over the heart of the plate. My bat connected and drove the ball between two outfielders. I slid into third base with a triple. As I dusted off my uniform and caught my breath, Valeo tipped his hat, grinned, and mouthed, "Attaboy."

My teammates cheered from the dugout. The game's outcome was on the line as Perkins stepped in the batter's box.

Everyone in the bleachers stood as the always confident Perkins held his bat high in his familiar stance. The tension mounted as teammates cheered him on. As Perkins dug his spikes into the dirt around the batter's box, he and the pitcher stared each other down, exchanging menacing glares. My teammates rooted for Perkins to hit the ball a long way. Valeo had other plans.

The first pitch brushed Perkins off the plate.

The umpire howled, "Strike one!"

Perkins argued the pitch was inside. The umpire yanked off his mask to warn him to stop complaining before he tossed him from the game. Rather than push his luck over a bad call, Perkins dug in and waited.

Valeo took his time before his next delivery. Was he afraid to throw the pitch, or did he want to give Perkins something to think about?

Perkins stepped out of the batter's box. "Let's go, Valeo. Throw the ball. We don't have all day."

The tension mounted as Perkins took his stance and waited for the next pitch. Perkins took a mighty swing as he landed on one knee, nearly corkscrewing himself into the ground.

"Strike two!" the umpire wailed.

"No need to do too much, Lenny," our manager called out. "A single will tie the score."

Perkins spat on the ground and waggled his bat. He was going to send the next pitch into orbit. Valeo began his windup and delivered his best fastball. High and outside. Just where Perkins likes it. He always crushes pitches in his happy zone. His body twisted like a pretzel. Cheers came from one dugout, groans from the other. A flying bat slammed against the backstop.

The umpire roared, "Strike three. You're out. Ballgame over."

I'll never forget the pitch grooved to a kid with low self-esteem. Destined to let my teammates down, a hero stepped in and saved my dignity. If not for Johnny's insight, I would have crashed and burned, retreating deeper into my cocoon. How could anyone so young sense my struggle with confidence? Somehow, he did.

A half-century later, I still recall the events of that day. To most, it was just another meaningless game. To me, it meant so much more.

When I learned of John Valeo's death, I reached out to his sister. Heart failure? How can a heart as big as Johnny's fail? I regret never thanking the boy with a man's vision that day. Not sure if he can hear me now, but thanks, Johnny.

HEART OF GLASS

Early December

Debbie knew she'd be a sounding board after she heard Michelle's pathetic voice on the telephone. *Here we go again. Will she ever learn?*

She called out to her husband. "Michelle has another crisis. She's on her way over."

"What now?" Nick asked.

"Louie the Loser dumped her. She needs a shoulder to cry on."

"And the advice she won't listen to."

"Be compassionate. Michelle's taking this one hard."

"Miss Drama Queen has been down that road too often. Why bother? She's not all there. One of these days, she'll snap. When she does, I don't want you anywhere near her."

"She's not a psychopath. Just a little mixed up."

"More than a little, Deb."

Screeching tires and a blasting horn announced Michelle's arrival.

"All she wants in life is to settle down with a family," Debbie said. "She's afraid time is running out. Despite her beauty, she attracts dirtbags."

"It's what's inside her head that scares good men off. No normal guy will put up with her jealousy and temper tantrums. I wish you'd stay away from her." The horn honked again. "You're being paged. Hurry out there before neighbors complain."

Debbie hadn't fastened her seat belt when Michelle's Corvette peeled from the curb. "Slow down, dammit! Before you get us killed."

Michelle ignored her friend's plea and continued to race down the street.

"It's for the best," Debbie said. "If you ask me, your breakup is a blessing. Louie's attraction to you was for one reason, and it wasn't love."

"I didn't ask you, did I?"

"Then why am I sitting in the passenger seat? Listen to me for once?"

"Here comes Mother Teresa's lecture."

"How many times have I told you not to jump into bed with every guy who walks into your life?"

"Like you didn't? You had a wild streak during your college days."

"We're talking about you right now. Besides, I was more selective. Tell me this? Did you ever hear of the word, *no*?"

Michelle floored the accelerator and swerved in and out of traffic. "I thought we had something special. Then just like that, it's over."

"You dated a month. Don't behave as if Louie was in your life forever."

"I thought Louie was different."

"He used you like every other guy."

"Don't scold me. I misjudged the prick's character. Why does shit always happen to me?"

"Because you allow it. I voiced my opinions about Louie when I first met him. You said I had him pegged wrong. Looks like I was right."

"You're always right, or so you think."

"Hey! I don't deserve this. I'm trying to talk sense into you. But as usual, you won't listen."

Michelle turned her eyes off the road for an instant. She gave Debbie a look of dismay before focusing on the road again. "I knew nothing was wrong until he shot one last load. He wasn't even soft yet when he complained I wasn't the type to get serious with. Guys. I'll never figure them out. The more they want, the more I give. The more I give, the more they want. Then when they tire of me, I'm discarded like an old toy and replaced with someone else to play with."

"If you wish to put out, that's your business, but you have a habit of going overboard."

Michelle ignored the red light when her Corvette approached the crowded intersection at Hempstead Turnpike and Merrick Avenue. She turned onto Hempstead Turnpike, cutting off oncoming traffic. With horns honking and tires screeching, Michelle flashed her middle finger to an irate motorist. At the corner, she made an illegal left without signaling into Borrelli's Restaurant parking lot. Debbie made the sign of the cross.

"Shit!" Michelle grunted as she slapped her open palm against the steering wheel. "What's his problem?"

"Who?"

"The fuckin' cop. He followed me into the parking lot." She studied the officer in the rearview mirror as he approached. "Watch this, Deb. It works every time." She unfastened the top buttons of her blouse to reveal her abundant cleavage. "Once he gets a peek at these babies, he'll put away his ticket book and flirt with me."

The officer tapped on her side window. He motioned to roll it down.

"Did I do something wrong, officer?"

"I clocked you doing seventy-five in a forty, ma'am. And let us not forget the half-dozen other infractions."

"Today has not been a good day for me, officer."

"Your day is about to get worse. License and registration, please."

"Will you take a phone number instead? I'm between boyfriends, and you have no wedding ring on your finger. Let's work something out."

"Not interested, lady. For the last time, license and registration."

"Don't you have anything better to do than sit on the side of the road, waiting to nab someone for a traffic violation? It's nine o'clock. Shouldn't you be at the doughnut shop?"

"Another word, and you'll find yourself handcuffed in the back of the patrol car."

"Ooh, sounds kinky."

"Shut up," interrupted Debbie. "Give the officer what he wants."

Michelle held her blouse wide open to allow him an unobstructed view of her prize possessions. "Is this what you want, Mr. Policeman? This is your lucky day. I'm not wearing a bra."

"Put them away. Propositioning a police officer is reason to take you to the station."

"Why the station? Didn't you suggest handcuffs and taking me into your backseat? It's not too romantic, but it sounds exciting."

"What did I say about propositioning me? Don't you listen?"

In a seductive voice, she whispered, "Are you going to spank me for being bad?"

"That's enough, lady. Step out of the car. Place your hands on the hood."

"Is this where you frisk me and take me into your backseat?"

"This is where I arrest you and take you to the station."

Debbie rushed to her friend's aid, hoping to convince the officer to forget Michelle's insanity. He looked familiar. She moved closer to read the name on the uniform. "I don't believe it. It's Ken Tomkins. It's me, Debbie Carpenter. Hofstra University."

"Debbie. I can't believe it. It's been twenty years. You look great. You haven't aged a day. The last time I saw you, we snuck away from that graduation party to put the backseat of my Ford Bronco to good use. So, what have you been up to?"

"I'm an English teacher at East Meadow High School." She held out her left hand to show her wedding ring. "I settled down years ago. How about you?"

"Haven't found the right woman yet."

Michelle jumped into the conversation. "Small world, officer. I haven't found my match either. Looks like we can kill two birds with one stone if we hook up?"

His patience running thin, Ken glanced at Debbie. "Where did you find this one?"

"She's an emotional wreck tonight. I'm trying to talk sense into her."

"She needs a psychiatrist, not an English teacher."

"I'm not crazy," Michelle cried out. "I seldom behave like this, but when my heart is broken how it was today, I do stupid things."

Debbie directed her comments toward Ken. "Michelle's next birthday will be her fortieth. She's still barhopping. I've told her a hundred times, it's not the place to find a meaningful relationship, but she doesn't listen."

"What am I supposed to do, Deb? As much as I'm tired of getting hurt, I can't give up and accept all the good men are taken. Mr. Right is out there somewhere. I won't find him if I stay home at night feeling sorry for myself."

Officer Tomkins tucked his ticket book into his back pocket. "Against my better judgment and as a favor for Debbie, I won't issue the tickets you deserve. But, if I ever catch you driving how you were tonight, you won't be so lucky." He gestured toward her exposed breasts. "It's cold out here. Button up."

"Don't worry about these suckers. With the crap they've gone through, it'll take more than weather elements to knock the life out of them."

"Michelle! Shut up, already." Debbie turned to Ken and apologized for her friend's outburst. "Thanks for not writing her up. I owe you one."

"I'll pay my own debts," Michelle said as she locked eyes with the officer. "Dinner sometime? My treat."

"Are you soliciting me again?"

"I promise to keep my clothes on. Unless you take them off."

"I'll tell you what I'll do. I'll take you up on your dinner proposal, but don't get any ideas. This is not a date. My purpose is to talk sense into you."

"Save your breath, Ken," Debbie interrupted. "If she won't listen to her best friend, she sure as heck won't listen to a stranger."

"I took a psychology course while in college. After being on the force for eighteen years, it helps me understand people better. I've come across too many instances where women like Michelle destroy their lives. Their future might have turned out differently if they had someone to talk to, other than friends who misguide them. Unfortunately, I've seen it happen too many times. Some hit the bottle, others turn to drugs or prostitution. If I can spend time in a relaxed environment, there's a chance I can get through to her."

"Good luck, Ken. Listening is not Michelle's strong point."

"What do you know, Deb? Officer Tomkins wears a uniform. He carries himself with authority. I love men in uniforms. If he wants to tell me something, he's got my attention." She turned to Ken. "What time and where?"

"Why not at here at Borrelli's? I'm off duty on Sunday. How does six o'clock work?"

"Perfect. But dinner is on me."

"Let me remind you. I'm not expecting anything in return. Just so you don't get any ideas, you pay for your meal. I'll pay for mine."

"Have it your way, Officer Tomkins, but the dessert is on me."

Ken rolled his eyes.

"Listen, Ken," Debbie said. "Michelle has a heart of glass. If this goes anywhere beyond dinner, please promise you won't hurt her."

Michele whispered in Ken's ear. "Do you hear that, good-looking? I'm fragile."

***

Six months later, Debbie and Nick discussed what a different person Michelle had become since meeting Ken.

Debbie laughed. "She was in rare form that night. I'm surprised Ken took her up on the dinner proposal and how well they connected."

"We know what happened, Deb. Michelle took care of dessert and filled his sweet tooth."

"Whatever she did, she's fortunate a good man came into her life to help screw her head on right."

"Michelle is Michelle. Just wait."

"Sounds like you expect disaster."

"It's just a matter of time," Nick answered.

***

Last week of June

Late Friday after lunchtime, coworkers Judy Madison and Donna Zimmer entered Michelle's office.

"Excuse us," Donna said. "Do you have a minute? We want to run something by you."

"Sure, girls. Is anything wrong?"

"Looks that way. It's none of our business, but you need a heads up."

Judy began. "I ran into Ken at Majors Steak House during lunchtime yesterday and thought about walking

96

over to say hello, but he was with someone. I didn't want to intrude. Whoever his companion was, they were enjoying each other's company. I heard their laughter across the room."

Michelle explained. "Ken mentioned something about catching up with one of his retired precinct buddies for lunch. Cops get noisy when they're together."

"Are you sure she was a cop?"

"She? Ken's guest was a woman?"

"Not the bra-buster you are, but with her looks, she'd have no trouble finding a man to join her in the bedroom."

Donna added, "As I do every Friday, I scoot out before lunch and pick up pizzas at Borrelli's for the office girls. I was early. The pies weren't ready yet. During my wait, I saw Ken sitting in a booth with a woman who fit the same description as the one Judy saw yesterday. Ken and I hung out with the same crowd during high school. He's not aware we work together. After small talk, he introduced his lunch companion as his dear friend, Debbie. She looked familiar. They left Borelli's at the same time as me. I saw her drive away in a green Miata."

Michelle's fingers ran through her long blond hair. "My best friend, Debbie, drives a green Miata." She clenched her fist—pain shot through her heart. Something was going on between her best friend and the man she'd been living with for four months. Ken seemed different from the others. She'd thought the same about Louie. Look where that got her.

"Does this Debbie work in the area?" Judy asked.

"She's a schoolteacher. Off for the summer."

"Ah, so that's it. With so much spare time during the summer recess, a sizzling affair is a fun way to cure the boredom."

"Judy!" snapped Donna. "We don't know what the deal is. Don't put any thoughts in Michelle's head."

"It's obvious. That woman was hot. Ken and his female companion are sleeping together."

Michelle's hands covered her face. Tears squeezed between her fingers, dripping onto a stack of papers on her desk.

***

"Why are you so quiet tonight?" Ken asked as he and Michelle sat at the kitchen table having dinner.

"Just have a lot on my mind. I learned some disturbing news at the office today."

"Can I help with anything?"

"It's confidential. I'll work it out." She changed the subject and mentioned not hearing from Debbie in a while. "I wonder if she's avoiding me for a reason?"

Ken stood from the table, still chewing his food. "It's getting late. I need to get ready for work."

"What's the rush, Kenneth? Why leave food on your plate? It's early. You don't leave the house for another two hours. Don't you like my cooking?"

"Your cooking is fine. It's just that I need to get in early to catch up on the red tape I've put off longer than I should have. You know how it is." He planted a kiss on her forehead and headed toward the shower.

Michele talked to herself as soon as Ken closed the bathroom door. "Yeah, I know how it is. You're avoiding the conversation about not seeing Debbie in a while."

When the water ran, she scrolled the caller list on Ken's phone. Listed was an incoming call from his mother and two outgoing calls to Debbie's cell. Michelle mumbled. "You are messing with the wrong broad."

She dialed Debbie's phone, pretending just to chat. During their call, there was no hint of lunch dates with Ken. The conversation ended with Debbie saying, "It's been so hectic around here. We haven't seen you guys in a month. Let's get together soon. Tell Ken I said hello."

After Ken left for work, Michelle opened a bottle of Kendall Jackson to drown herself in sorrow. Why is she always the one to get hurt? And how could her trusted friend betray her?

Ken sat in his patrol car on the side of the road aiming his radar gun at cars going by in a school zone. He dialed Debbie on the cell to arrange this afternoon's get-together.

"We might have a problem," Debbie warned. "The classmate you chatted with at Borrelli's looked familiar. I could be wrong, but I may have met her at Michelle's barbecue last summer. What if she recognized me and said something to Michelle?"

"Don't be paranoid."

"I have bad vibes on this. Michelle was distant during our phone call last night. She phoned me. Yet, she had little to say. It's not like her."

"Come to think of it, she mentioned you avoiding her."

"Hope she's not on to us? I'd feel like crap if she found out what we are up to."

"She's preoccupied with a problem at work. She has no clue."

"As a precaution, let's meet at my house this afternoon. On the way over, stop off at Borrelli's and pick up a pizza. Nick won't be home until after six. Park in the garage in case she snoops around during her lunch hour."

**

Ken suggested using his uncle's summer cottage on Shelter Island to celebrate Independence Day and Michelle's birthday at the same time. They'd sit on the beach and watch the fireworks display with a bottle of champagne. She'd prefer to celebrate her fortieth birthday at a fancy restaurant in Manhattan. But Ken already made plans. The more she thought about it, the better she liked his idea.

Ken pulled his car in front of the cottage. A surge of fireworks made it sound like a war zone.

"Someone is starting the celebration early," he said as Michelle stepped from the passenger seat.

She studied the surroundings. "How 'bout we take a short walk to stretch our legs?"

"Later. I'm eager to go inside."

Not listening to Ken, she strolled toward the high beach grass. Ken followed.

"I love it, Ken. It's isolated, within walking distance of the cottage, and fifty feet from the beach. Just what I'm looking for. The perfect place to do it."

"Sounds like a plan. We'll cross that bridge later."

"Let's cross it now. No more secrets."

"What secrets?"

"I'm not a dumb blonde. I know what's going on. You and Debbie are meeting secretly behind my back."

"Dammit! I noticed you've been standoffish lately and had a feeling you knew something was up. We did our best to get together discreetly. Somehow you figured it out."

"I've had enough surprises to last a lifetime. I can't take another one."

"It was Debbie's idea."

"I'm sure the slut didn't have to twist your arm."

"Whoa. Where'd that come from?"

"I know what's going on between you two." Her hands trembled as she pulled Ken's service revolver from her pocketbook.

"What the ...?"

Two gunshots blended in with the exploding fireworks. Ken fell to the ground.

"That'll teach you not to stick your dick where it doesn't belong," Michelle said, as the holiday explosions stopped for a moment. "I am the first to admit, Debbie is a hot number. Is she worth dying for?"

Ken gasped his final breaths. "Nothing is going on between us," he moaned in a voice not much louder than a whisper.

"Bullshit. Try again, lover boy. Remember when you followed me into Borrelli's parking lot? You and Deb reminisced about what went on in the backseat of your Bronco years ago. I never expected you'd renew acquaintances."

"We were only..."

"You were only getting a piece of Debbie's ass when I wasn't around. But my best friend? Go to hell!" She fired another bullet.

Ken tried to speak but choked on his own blood as she ranted on with her suspicions. "The two closest people in my life betrayed me. Why?" She aimed between Ken's legs. She pulled the trigger. "Ouch. That's gotta hurt as much as you hurt me." She stood over Ken as he lay motionless, his breathing labored. She rifled through his pockets, took his cash, and tossed the wallet into tall beach grass to make it appear like a robbery. "I'll watch you die and wait an hour before I call your cell. Tonight, I'll dial 911, put on the worried girlfriend act, and explain you went out for wine and never returned."

She would have continued bragging about her perfect murder, but Ken wasn't listening. He was dead.

Michelle's plan was to head to the cottage, clean her fingerprints from the gun, and toss the weapon into the sound. After she threw her clothes into the washing machine, she'd take a long hot shower to remove the evidence of ever being on the beach. Police will see her as a grieving girlfriend instead of a cold-blooded murderer.

She staggered to the front door and took a deep breath before opening it. Holding the gun in her right hand, she flipped on the light switch with her left. Taking two steps inside, she saw dozens of balloons with birthday greetings on them. A second later, a large crowd of friends and family greeted her with, *"Surprise! Happy Birthday."*

Debbie rushed over and embraced her good friend. "It took Ken and me a month to plan this party. It wasn't easy without causing suspicion. I bet you didn't expect this." She looked around. "Where's Ken?"

"Hey, Michelle?" Nick asked. "What's with the gun?"

CRYSTAL'S SECRET

Mark cleaned up his disheveled appearance, wanting to make a good impression. During their unexpected phone conversation, he learned how successful Crystal had become. He couldn't allow her to see him as an unemployed failure. Their lives had gone in different directions. He could jot down his accomplishments inside a matchbook cover, while Crystal's life made for a full-length motion picture.

As Mark waited at the arrival gate, he didn't know what to expect. Their relationship ended on a sour note twenty-five years ago, and he questioned her motive for wanting to meet him. Despite thousands of faceless people in the crowded airport, it didn't take long for two sets of eyes to find each other. On the plus side of forty and still a looker, Crystal's body language hinted something disturbing was happening in her life.

They rushed into each other's arms and locked lips with a kiss that lasted much too long for distant friends. Dare he tell her not a day had gone by that she wasn't in his thoughts? Should he ask why she broke his heart, or should he not open old wounds?

They walked through the airport, arm-in-arm, clinging together the same way they did as teenagers. Mark suggested a restaurant overlooking the Atlantic. In the romantic setting, the former couple tapped wine glasses in a toast to old friends. "It's been too long, Crystal. We have so much to catch up on."

"More than you can imagine, but this is not the time to get into specifics. What I need is a shoulder to cry on."

"Are you sick?"

"No, no, no. Let's just say I have a lot on my plate right now."

"Care to discuss it?"

"I'd rather talk about us and the days when life wasn't so complicated." She reached for his hand and squeezed hard. "I made a mistake a quarter-century ago and shouldn't have listened to my parents."

"Your parents had good reason not to like me. They believed you could do better than a long-haired high school dropout who cared more about his musical ambitions than finding a job. They did everything possible to split us apart, wanting what was best for their daughter."

"It was my future. I was old enough to make my own decisions. Who I choose to spend the rest of my life with was my business?"

"Love is blind, Crystal. You failed to see my shortcomings. Your parents did. If we stayed together, I would have taken you down with me."

"Why say that?"

A lump formed in Mark's throat. "We've always been honest with each other? So, whatever I tell you, please don't turn your back on me."

"Unless you're a child molester or serial killer, I'm sure I can forgive you."

"Nothing like that, but two years after we split, I self-destructed with a heroin addiction."

Crystal gasped, "I don't believe it. You were always against drug use."

"I'm clean now. Twenty years. After rehab, I ditched my guitar and became a writer. Another dream unfulfilled. I had three goals in life and achieved none of them. Chasing rock stardom nearly killed me. The famous author bit left me collecting welfare. Building a family with the most wonderful woman on earth ended with a broken heart." Before Crystal responded, he continued. "You've had a successful career. If you had stayed with me, you wouldn't have become who you are. Dumping me was a smart move."

"Who am I, Mark? When I look in the mirror, I don't recognize the face staring back at me. I'm not who you think I am, nor am I the person I want to be. You don't know the compromises I made to achieve my success. I'd give it up for that log cabin in the mountains of Pennsylvania we dreamed of as teenagers. Away from the nightmares that wake me up each night, away from ..." When her voice trailed off, Mark pressured her to continue. She only added, "I've done stuff I'm not proud of."

"Everyone has skeletons. I told you about my drug addiction."

"When you self-destructed, you hurt only yourself. You were man enough to fight off the demons and turn your life around. My greed and hunger for the almighty dollar hurt thousands of people and their families. No matter what I do to make amends, the damage is irreversible. It's something I can't forgive myself for." She gazed at Mark with sadness in her eyes. "If we stayed together, I'd be a lot better off today."

"I doubt it. We would have struggled financially. What could I have given you that would make you happy?"

She tried to hold back a smile but couldn't. "You already gave it to me, Mark. Which is why you're a big part of my life, even if we haven't been together in twenty-five years."

"What have I given you?"

"When the time comes, you'll know."

"Damn it! You've talked in circles from the minute we met at the airport. You said you needed a shoulder to cry on, yet you won't tell me why you're crying. What's with the secrecy? Why are we here?"

"Isn't it enough to just want to see you again?" She threw a kiss across the table. "So, what's the plan? Do I check myself into a hotel and spend my one day in town alone? Or will you invite me to stay the night at your apartment?"

Her suggestion caught Mark by surprise. "You're married. I don't want you to do something you might regret."

"The offer is out there, Mark. Take advantage of it. If I don't turn you on anymore, just say so."

Before saying goodbye at the airport the following morning, Mark tried again to have Crystal answer the questions she sidestepped the night before. Her vagueness only left more questions, which made her more mysterious than when she first walked through the arrival gate.

"Can we meet again?" Mark asked.

"No."

"Oh, geez! I hope you are not second-guessing yourself for what went on last night, and you're disappointed in me?"

"No way, Mark. I'll cherish our get-together for the rest of my life. You are the best thing that ever happened to me. If there was a way to have you in my life again, I'd do it in a heartbeat."

"Please, Crystal. If the passion you displayed in the bedroom last night was real, why vanish from my life again?"

"I'll write to explain when I get home. I need to do something before I answer the questions I've avoided. You deserve an explanation. But it'll be impossible to see you again."

"Is that your final answer?" he joked, mimicking Regis Philbin on *Who Wants to Be a Millionaire*.

"Very final."

Teary-eyed, she kissed him even more passionately than when they first met at the airport. "I love you," was all she said as she turned and walked away without looking back.

Three days later, when Mark arrived home from the unemployment office, he opened his mailbox. Inside sat an envelope postmarked California, with only Crystal's first name written in the upper left-hand corner.

> *Dear Mark,*
>
> *Thank you for the lovely weekend and for making me feel like a woman again. As much as I didn't want to return to California, I had no choice. Involved in a world of sin, I wanted out but was in too deep. Escaping my environment would endanger the lives of my loved ones. I knew enough to bring down an empire, which made it impossible to*

walk away. No matter where I hid, they would find me.

My autobiography is complete. I'm counting on you, my favorite author, to write the epilogue. You know how I love happy endings. Do what you can to make it so.

I left a suitcase in the back of your closet. Inside is enough cash to set you up for life. Not to mention a deed in your name for an acre of lakefront property with a log cabin in the Pocono Mountains. Just what we always wanted. Enjoy. I'm aware of your struggles to find a job, but that's okay. You made a wrong turn along your journey, but you're on the right road now.

The less you know of the underground world I'm part of or the countless lives I destroyed, the safer it is. I can blame my husband and claim I went along for the ride, but once the money rolled in, I became the same monster he was.

Rather than expose my young daughter to the business, I passed Heather off to my sister. Enclosed is Heather's contact info. I'm leaving it to you to explain why I abandoned her. Put a good word in for me.

Inside the suitcase is a large manila envelope with bank accounts, CDs, and money markets in my daughter's name. I should've mentioned Heather sooner, but it wasn't the time. But you need to know. Figure out the math. I gave birth six months after our breakup. I regret not telling you, but my parents brainwashed me into hiding the pregnancy and staying with my sister until after the baby's birth.

I reached a point where I couldn't deal with the guilt of destroying people's lives anymore. The madness had to stop. The only way out was to take the bastard I called my husband with me. When you read this letter, I'll be dead. But please, Mark, don't mourn my loss. Instead, celebrate your gain. Look toward the future. I bet my life you'll do what's right and become the father Heather never had. I love you and always have.

    Crystal

PUMPKIN

I've been on a sabbatical from the real world after the accident took my wife's life. Each day runs into the next. It's been a week without her. Words can't express how sorry I am for what happened. Stephanie deserved a better fate. I'd give anything if it were me buried instead of her.

I amble across the spacious field lined with gravesites decorated with mementos. A young couple cry as they place a teddy bear against a headstone. Fifty yards farther, an old man supported by a walker stands alone near a fresh grave while a group of younger people wait behind.

Autumn winds whip through the cemetery to make it feel colder than it is. But not as cold as my life has been since that dreaded day. I replaced the wilted carnations laid last week with fresh ones and said the usual prayers. I nod to a woman who left a basket of candy at a nearby headstone.

A teenage girl with straggly hair and circles under her eyes, wearing cut-off jeans and a t-shirt with a pumpkin logo, approaches me. She whispers, "Death is hard to accept."

I motion toward Stephanie's burial plot. "My wife. It wasn't her time."

"Same with Christine," she said, pointing at the gravesite four headstones away. "Only seventeen. Every Halloween, her mom leaves a bowl of candy next to her tombstone. It's her way of dealing with her daughter's death."

"Yes, I saw the woman. She walked right by me as if I weren't there. I nodded and said hello, but she didn't respond."

"Don't mind her. She lives in a different world than us."

Bill gazed into her eyes. "I have to give you credit. This is one great makeup job. The gray skin, the sunken eyes. You look so dead. Are you attending a Halloween bash later this evening?"

"I was about to call it a night when you arrived."

"It's eight o'clock, young lady. When I was your age, the night had just begun."

"I partied enough to last a lifetime. My wild and crazy days are long gone."

"Then what's with the great costume?"

"It's a long story."

"I'd love to hear it." He reached out his hand. "Bill Winters. I'm pleased to meet you."

"Same here, Bill. I just wish we were meeting under different circumstances. My friends and family call me Pumpkin. Born on Halloween."

"Happy Birthday, Pumpkin."

"Yeah, right? On my birthday, Mom accused me of stealing the money she kept hidden under the computer keyboard. I swear, I didn't take it."

"Did you tell her that?"

"She didn't believe me. I ran from the house. As always, when it didn't go my way, I escaped reality by getting high. She hasn't seen me since."

"Have you tried to contact her?"

"If I could walk through the door and say, 'Mom, I'm home,' I would, but it's too late."

"It's never too late. The longer you put it off, the harder it gets. You need to straighten this mess out."

Just then, a group of zombies, ghosts, and skeletons rushed through the graveyard and stole the bowl of candy from Pumpkin's friend's headstone. I yelled, "Leave that candy where it is, you bastards."

"Don't get upset, Bill. It's okay. Every year the kids take the candy. Christine doesn't have a sweet tooth anymore."

"It's not the point. Today's kids have no freaking manners. Bill stopped to rephrase his quote. 'Not all kids.' You are living proof the younger generation still has promise."

"Man. Do you have me pegged wrong. You're not aware of my heroin addiction and reputation. Nobody mistook me for the Virgin Mary. My lifestyle put Mom through hell."

"Everybody makes mistakes. Believe me, I know. Are you still into drugs?"

"No way! I'm clean and haven't slept with anyone in years."

"Good girl. Your mom would be proud."

"It doesn't matter anymore."

"It sure as heck does. Where does your mom live?"

"Around the block."

"Pumpkin? You're so close."

"Yet so far away, Bill."

"Let's visit your mom and straighten this mess out. This has gone on long enough."

"Can't do it as much as I wish I could. I can't leave the cemetery."

"Will you turn into a pumpkin if you do?"

"Something like that."

"I get it. You're dead. I'm talking to a ghost. Ha, ha, ha. Trick or treat."

Sad, empty eyes stared back at me as the full moon glowed like a spotlight on Stephanie's grave. "You need to know, Bill. I'm in the same boat as you. Except I've been rowing aimlessly for a much longer time. After seeing you caught in the same trap as me, I realized we need to accept our fate."

"What trap?"

"Denial," she answered.

"Denial of what?"

She led me by the hand to her friend's tombstone and read the inscription.

Christine Harrison
Born October 31, 1999
Died October 31, 2016

"It's time for you and Christine to rest in peace."

"I don't understand. Who is Christine?"

"Me. This is my home. I've been drifting between two worlds since I died of a drug overdose."

"This is getting scary. You sound so convincing."

She pointed at my wife's plot. "When the granite headstone replaces the temporary cross that now marks this grave, it will have two names on it. This is your denial."

"Denial of what, and why two names?"

"I know about the accident that killed your wife."

"You weren't there. How would you know?"

"You can't run away from this any longer, Bill. I watched cemetery workers lower two caskets in the ground on this spot last week. Your wife isn't alone. You're dead, Bill. You died in the accident with Stephanie. She forgives you when you drove home drunk that night after the party. Don't wander aimlessly for years like I did. She's waiting for you. Join her. It's time to get on with death."

LITTLE GIRL LOST

Mary drove her red pickup truck through the lot twice before spotting the open space in the next aisle. It was the morning before Christmas. Parking spaces were at a minimum.

She hit the gas pedal and zipped around the lane, beating the Cadillac, aiming for the same spot. The angry driver leaned on his horn and yelled, "You took my parking space, you idiot."

"And a Merry Christmas to you too," Mary shouted back.

The Cadillac driver flipped her the bird before he sped off, leaving a patch of rubber behind.

The confrontation put Mary on edge. Hearing the background music playing *'Tis the Season to Be Jolly* as she entered Walmart didn't restore her Christmas spirit. "For crying out loud," Sally complained to herself. "The store just opened, and it's already packed with last-minute holiday shoppers."

Her husband played Santa for the grandkids on Christmas Day for ages. This year, she had the idea that it would be a fun touch if she dressed up as Mrs. Santa. Aware the crowds would increase as the hours passed, her goal was to pick up the Mrs. Santa costume and escape the store before the crowd trampled her.

Mary did her best to avoid the obnoxious shoppers as they pushed through the crowd like defensive linebackers. And then it happened. A customer in an electric cart rammed into her ankle. The searing pain made her lash out at the old geezer with an onslaught of unladylike words. Mary thought *this was going to be one of those days*. Regretting her outburst, she blamed herself for waiting until the last day to go shopping. *What else will go wrong to kill the Christmas spirit?*

Not looking forward to another rear-end collision, she hobbled to a less crowded aisle to rub her aching ankle. As she tried to massage the pain away, she turned toward the sound of a child's whimper.

"What's wrong, honey?"

The little girl held out her arms. "Where did she go?"

"If you're looking for your mommy, I'm sure she's looking for you too."

"Mommy isn't here. She's not coming back."

"Let's backtrack. Where were you when you last saw her?"

She sniffled and pointed toward the grocery department.

Mary led her through the store. As they passed the sports section, the child stopped to stare in awe at the pink bicycle on display. "I have my cousin's old junkie boy bike, with the bar in the middle. I hate it."

"Maybe Santa will deliver a new one tonight."

"I don't believe in him anymore. Sue Ann says Santa's a fake."

"If he's fake, who is the guy with the red suit and white beard in front of the store?"

"Sue Ann says Walmart pays him to dress like that."

"Don't believe everything Sue Ann says."

"She's smart. Seven and a half. She should know."

"I'm smart too and a whole lot older than Sue Ann. I know more about Santa than she does." She placed her hand on the child's shoulders. "I'm Mrs. McKay. And you?"

"Denise Cunningham. I'm six years old. I live in the white house across the street from the Super Scoop ice cream store."

"Wow. You are so lucky. Yummy."

"I'd take a new bike over ice cream any day."

An announcement came over the intercom.

Attention shoppers: Be on the lookout for six-year-old Denise. With shoulder-length light brown hair and a missing front tooth, Denise is wearing blue jeans and a Mickey Mouse T-shirt. If anybody sees her, please bring her to the Customer Service Department.

"There you go. Your mother is waiting for you. Let's go find her." Mary held Denise's hand as they cut through the crowded aisles on their way to Customer Service. Before they got there, Denise broke away from Mary's grip and rushed to a tall woman with long blond hair looking at Christmas cards. She clutched onto her leg. "Mommy, Mommy. Why did you go away and leave me?"

The woman peeled the child from her leg to break free. "I'm sorry, honey. I'm not your mother."

Mary rushed over to the woman. "If you're not her mother, why is she acting like you are?"

"I don't know. I never saw this kid in my life."

Mary stared into the child's eyes. "Are you sure this is your mom?"

"I think so."

"Oh my God," a shorter woman with a darker complexion cried out as she rushed over and lifted Denise into her arms. "I'd never forgive myself if something happened to you."

The woman Denise mistook for her mother cut in, "Not for nothing, lady, but you need to keep a closer eye on the kid. You can't allow her to roam around a crowded store unsupervised."

"I was watching her. She wandered off when I turned my attention for less than a minute to pick out a roast."

Believing the lady with the blond hair would continue her lecture, Mary said, "It's okay. I got this."

As the stranger drifted away, Denise's mother introduced herself as Lisa Cunningham. She set the child down and embraced Mary. "Thank you for looking out for my daughter."

Denise cried out, "You're not my mother. You only live in our house because Daddy likes you."

With sad eyes, Lisa avoided Denise's harsh comment. "I married Denise's father earlier this year."

"I'm Mary McKay. A pleasure meeting you and a Merry Christmas."

"I can't thank you enough for looking out for Denise's safety."

"No big deal. I enjoyed the kid's company. This morning didn't start off too well, but she helped brighten my day."

Lisa turned to Denise. "How about we hit McDonald's food court on the way out?"

The child's face lit up. "I'll race you there." She pushed her way through the crowd.

With Denise far ahead, Lisa joked, "I better keep up before I lose her again. Please join us."

Mary's throbbing ankle told her to pick up the Mrs. Claus costume and hit the checkout counter. Curiosity said to hang around a while longer. The two women sat at a table while Denise waited in line for her Kiddie Meal.

"It's none of my business, Lisa, but can I ask why Denise mistook the woman at the card section for her mother?"

Lisa looked up to make sure her daughter hadn't wandered off again. "Denise's mom died in a car accident on Christmas Eve two years ago. She was out doing last-minute shopping. Denise has had difficulty dealing with her mom's death and can't accept her leaving without saying goodbye. The woman in the card section had an uncanny resemblance to Judy. Denise may have thought her birth mother came back." She removed a tissue from her purse and wiped her damp eyes. "I'm not sure if she'll ever accept me."

"These things take time, Lisa. She'll come around."

"As hard as I try to reach her, she rejects me. In Denise's eyes, I'm a full-time nanny. She has never called me Mommy. I'm doing everything I can to make her think of me as her mother, but it's just not working." Lisa wiped tears from her eyes. "I don't know what to try next."

"Oh, dear. I'm so sorry." Mary whispered, "Is Santa delivering her a new bicycle tonight?"

"She already has one."

"I heard about her cousin's hand-me-down boys' bike. She hates it, Lisa."

"How do you know about that?"

"Denise told me all about it when she stopped to look at the display model in the bike section. You know how kids are. Peer pressure. Does her friend Sue Ann have a new bike?"

"Yes, if I remember correctly, she got one for her birthday during the summer. Denise wasn't even riding yet."

"If you can swing it, Walmart has an assembled pink bike on display at a sale price."

"She just learned to ride a month ago. It's much too soon. Besides, we spent more than we could afford on her already. By next year, our finances should improve."

Mary stood to leave. "I understand. Excuse me. I need to finish my shopping. I have an item or two I need to pick up. Have a Merry Christmas."

The two women embraced, and Mary limped over to Denise. "Don't give up on Santa just yet. Sue Ann doesn't know what she's talking about." She hobbled through the crowd, the shooting pain in her ankle worse than ever.

***

Denise unwrapped her presents on Christmas morning but lacked the enthusiasm and excitement one would expect from a six-year-old. Instead, she sat quietly drawing images of a bicycle Santa didn't deliver on her Etch-A-Sketch.

Noticing his daughter's withdrawal, her dad joined her on the couch. "We both miss Mommy. Christmas isn't the same without her. It's a big change for everyone. If Mommy could be with us now, she'd give the greatest gift of all."

"A bicycle?"

"No, silly. She'd give her love."

Denise shrugged. "I'm going outside to try out my Hula Hoop." Seconds later, Denise shrieked. "Come look, Daddy. My bicycle, my bicycle! I got my bicycle! And it's pink, just like the one in the store."

Her parents rushed outside. A bicycle decorated with a red ribbon and an envelope taped to the seat sat on the front lawn.

"Lisa? Why didn't you tell me about this?"

"Bruce. I had nothing to do with it. I'm as surprised as you are."

"Just great. Now I have to break the bad news and explain Santa made a mistake." He called Denise over and kneeled at eye level with his daughter. "Not sure what happened, sweetie, but Santa delivered the bike to the wrong address."

"No, he didn't. It's mine, it's mine!"

Lisa opened the envelope and read the note inside. Her voice cracked as tears ran down her face. "Bruce. You gotta read this. It's from Santa, addressed to Denise."

Denise looked up. "What does it say, Daddy?"

Dear Denise. With so many boys and girls giving me their Christmas lists, I forgot to unload your bicycle when I delivered all your other toys. Your stepmother sent me a text late last night asking me where it was. When I told her of my error, she begged me to turn around. She told me how much she loves you and how important it was for you to have a new, shiny bike this Christmas. I was halfway to the North Pole, but because she said what a special girl you were, I turned around to deliver it. Sorry for the mix-up. Hope you enjoy it. Merry Christmas, Santa.

Denise clapped her hands and climbed on the bicycle. "Mrs. McKay was right. There *is* a Santa Claus."

The puzzled parents watched their daughter peddle down the driveway and onto the sidewalk. "Mommy.

I'm going to Sue Ann's. I have proof that Santa Claus is real. And I can't wait to tell her how you got him to deliver my bicycle."

Tears clouded Lisa's eyes. "She called me *Mommy*."

Noticing his neighbor outside, Bruce trotted over and asked if he saw anyone deliver the bicycle.

"Sure did, Bruce. An older couple wearing red suits lined with white fur, black boots, and hats with pom-poms. He had a long white beard."

"Mr. and Mrs. Santa Claus?"

"A brilliant idea. I like the touch. I could see the glow in your daughter's eyes from next door. She hasn't smiled like that since Judy died."

"Miracles like this don't just happen. I suppose they came in a sleigh and flying reindeer?"

"Not that dramatic. Just a red pickup truck."

"I don't know anyone with a pickup."

"If it means anything, Mrs. Claus walked with a limp."

PUPPY LOVE

Every time I hear Cher's song, *If I Could Turn Back Time*, I think of the biggest mistake of my life. How I wish I could turn back time and change the way things worked out. Life offers no do-overs. The best I can do is learn from my mistake and move on. But where do I move on to? Caitlyn is no longer here.

The dictionary defines a teenager's first romance as puppy love—a coming-of-age encounter when two adolescents feel intimate emotions for each other. According to grownups, puppy love is an infatuation. Adolescents are incapable of the actual love adults experience. Caitlyn and I were the exception and shared affection, compassion, and intimacy the same way as mature adults. We were each other's best friend, each other's world.

It's not that she didn't give me time to take the next step. No other woman would have been so patient. High school sweethearts, we stayed together for ten beautiful years. All Caitlyn wanted was a ring on her finger to bond us together forever. I didn't get it.

Without an argument or bitter words, I did nothing to stop her when she warned, if I couldn't promise her a future, she'd find someone who would. If I were a man instead of the coward I was, I'd have realized how empty my life would be without her. Instead, I ignored her threat until it was too late.

Having a new man in her life, she had difficulty letting go of her former flame. Occasionally, we'd get together and behave like we were still an item. After sharing her love between two men longer than she should have, she couldn't continue going down this path. She had a choice to make and left it to me to decide. I'll never forget the rejected look in her eyes when I answered 'no' when she asked if there was any possibility of us getting back together?

Afraid of a lifetime commitment, I opened the door for someone else to step in and make his move. The lucky guy wasted little time. Within a year, he proposed. Why not? He knew perfection. I was the one who couldn't see the treasure in front of my eyes. She accepted, and I never expected to hear from her again because it's difficult for former lovers to remain casual friends. The times we spent together were beautiful memories I'll cherish forever.

Not long after her marriage, I became her sounding board when she needed to vent. Married life wasn't as rosy as expected. Who better to reach out to than the one person who understood her? When my words of wisdom weren't enough, we discarded the telephone nonsense and met face-to-face. Sometimes all she needed was a hug and me to convince her everything would work out. Other times, it got more complex, and a hug wasn't enough.

We said our farewells, whether on the phone or in person, the same way we had when two fifteen-year-old kids began dating. The word *goodbye* sounded too final. Instead, we used the more positive *later*.

Caitlyn spent the next few years mending problems at home. During that healing period, she gave birth to a daughter. She still phoned me, but not as often as before, although she never failed to call me on my birthday at noontime.

One day, when everything was going wrong at the office, the phone rang. I let the call go to the answering machine. Then I heard her voice. I picked up. "I'm having a bad day, Caitlyn. Can you call me tomorrow?"

Her voice quivered. "This can't wait. I just returned from the oncologist. It's not good."

She needn't say anything more. My business could wait. This was far more important. I once again became the glue that held her together.

We talked at length that day. By the end of our chat, the gloom and doom I heard earlier had changed to a more confident *I would beat this* attitude.

Following a courageous battle with countless chemo and radiation treatments, my girl walked away cured. She credited me for giving her the strength to go on. But it took a woman as strong as Caitlyn to spit in the devil's face and come out victorious.

How time flies. Now in our mid-forties, Caitlyn's turmoil at home had calmed down. Her daughter had just entered high school, and her checkups gave her a clean bill of health. I felt like her protective big brother who had guided his kid sister through the obstacles and roadblocks along her journey.

One day, she surprised me with a visit to my office. The solemn expression on her face said something was wrong. Before I could ask, she clung to me with all her strength and bawled her eyes out. We held the embrace until she ran out of tears. Then she spoke. Her cancer had returned. The disease was in a later stage than last time. She feared she'd lose the battle and couldn't face going through the awful treatments again. It sounded as if she had given up.

I encouraged her to be strong and assured her she would defeat this dreaded disease again. But how convincing was I when I broke down and cried?

I had been Caitlyn's emotional crutch for years. Now was not the time to abandon her, but I wasn't family. There wasn't much I could do apart from being a cheerleader on the sidelines.

During her drawn-out battle, our conversations were brief. Hearing her cancer was in remission made me so happy, and I wanted to take her to our once-favorite restaurant and celebrate. But with a husband in the picture, it wasn't possible.

She then spoke about her husband's support throughout her ordeal and how guilty she felt for neglecting him for so long. "Don't take this the wrong way. I've had your support from the beginning and have been the most loyal friend anyone can ask for. But I'm married. I shouldn't have depended on you so much."

In jest, I said, "Sounds like you're tired of me. Is this where you tell me to get out of your life?"

"Never happen. It's just that whatever is going on is between my husband and me. I shouldn't drag an old boyfriend into this mess."

"What mess?"

"Certain things are better off left unsaid."

If she wanted to volunteer the information, I'd listen, but I wouldn't twist her arm because it was none of my business. We ended the call on a positive note, and I wished her the best of luck. As we were about to hang up, we both said *later* at the same time.

Six months had gone by without contact with Caitlyn. I often thought of her and wanted to pick up the phone to hear her voice. But with her husband's irregular working hours, I couldn't take the chance he'd be home.

As I sat in my office, I noticed a woman stepping out of a taxi in the parking lot. I thought little of it until my secretary paged me. "A visitor in the lobby wants to meet with you. She said, "It was urgent.""

"I have a minute. Send her in."

When the woman walked into my office, I didn't recognize her right away. I did my best not to show my shock, but my voice cried out, "Oh,

"My god! Caitlyn! No!"

Her frail body made it clear the dreaded disease had returned. She had told me her cancer was in remission because she didn't want me to worry. As depressing as her outlook appeared, her spirits remained high.

Concerned about her future, I asked, "What is your next step."

She avoided the question. "I didn't come here today to talk about tomorrow. I'd prefer to recall our yesterdays and the great times we shared. Ah, to be young and healthy again."

Her laughter echoed off the office walls when she mentioned the time our canoe overturned in Belmont

Lake. I laughed along, but it was a charade because I was crying on the inside. We could have talked forever, but when the taxi returned to pick her up, I feared I'd never see her again.

During our walk to the parking lot, she turned more serious and let me know how much I'd meant to her. She then promised, no matter what happened, she'd call me on my birthday as she had every year since we were teenagers. We embraced farewell. I said our routine, "Later." She replied differently.

Two weeks later, her brother called with the news that left a hole in my heart. I thought of the last time we saw each other and understood why Caitlyn ended our final meeting with a formal '*goodbye.*'

When my birthday arrived a month after her death, the phone rang at noontime. Because of the timing, I thought of Caitlyn. I picked up the receiver to the sound of static. Then a dial tone. Did I have a poor connection, or had I received a call from heaven?

How am I doing so far? If possible, please leave an Amazon review after you finish reading. Giving reviews is something readers have no time to do anymore. It'll only take a minute. Reviews sell books and help with the Amazon ratings.

T.J. Hannon would also like to hear from you and learn your thoughts about Tales With a Twist at TJHANNONBOOKS@gmail.com.
What are your favorite stories? Least favorite?
TJ Hannon answers all emails. Thank you.

THE SHRINK

"Hello, Doctor Newman's office. Lucy speaking."

"Gotta speak to Doctor Newman."

"Sorry, sir. The doctor is with a patient. Can I help you?"

"My wife, Marlena Callahan, is his patient. I'm not happy with what's going down. Put him on the phone, now."

"Oh my. Sorry to learn of your dissatisfaction. Office hours end in fifteen minutes. Can I squeeze you in early tomorrow morning before sessions begin? You can discuss your issue with the doctor then. Does eight-thirty work for you?"

"What part of *now* don't you understand?"

"Sorry, Mr. Callahan, but the doctor can't see you today."

Lucy heard a click. Then a dial tone.

Twenty minutes later, a man rushed into the waiting room. "I'm George Callahan. Where the hell is he?"

Lucy stood from behind her desk. "You can't barge in here without an appointment. I told you Doctor Newman couldn't see you today."

"The doctor will see me. And he will see me now. So, get his ass out here."

"The office closed five minutes ago, Mr. Callahan. The doctor has an appointment after hours that he can't postpone."

"This won't take long. I'm not leaving till I see the scumbag."

Doctor Newman stepped from his office. "What's the commotion about?"

Lucy explained. "Mr. Callahan insists on seeing you."

"Is there a problem, Mr. Callahan?"

"Damn straight it is. That problem is you and your method of treatment for my wife."

Doctor Newman glanced at his watch. "It's after five o'clock, Lucy. I'll lock up. See you tomorrow."

As soon as Lucy left the building, the doctor invited George into his office.

"Please, take a seat, George."

"I'll stand, Doc. I won't be staying long."

Newman folded his arms across his chest and leaned against his desk. "What's the problem?"

"You tell me? My sister-in-law and I feared Marlena would do something stupid. She blamed herself for not watching our son closer when he fell into the swimming pool and drowned. I trusted your counseling would get her on the right track."

"Be patient. Your wife has come a long way."

"If that's the case, why has she lost interest in sex while under your care? With me anyway. Why is that?"

"Give her a little more time. I'm working on her progress."

"You're working on her all right."

"What are you getting at?"

"A good friend manages *The Dew Drop Inn* off Highway 42. A couple registered for a room last Friday night and stayed until wee hours the following morning. How convenient! I was away at a golf outing that weekend. From my friend's description, the woman looked like my wife. Her companion drove a blue Mercedes with a vanity license plate that said HEADDOC. Coincidently, the same color Mercedes and vanity plate as the one in your parking lot. Need I say anymore?"

The doctor broke out in laughter. "You caught us with our pants down. Guilty as charged. You'd find out soon enough."

"Don't laugh at me. This isn't funny."

"You don't understand. You got it all wrong."

George grabbed a letter opener from Newman's desk and shouted, "Sleeping with my wife, are you?" before plunging it into the doctor's neck, severing his carotid artery. The doctor fell to the ground and bled out onto the plush white carpet. George tucked the murder weapon into his back pocket and ran to his car. As he got to the parking lot, he saw his sister-in-law pull her Honda into the space next to him.

"Anita? What are you doing here?"

"I was about to ask you the same."

"I asked first. Are you a patient?"

"Hell no. Fred and I have a dinner date." She looked her brother-in-law in the eyes. "You look nervous. What's wrong?"

Ignoring her question, he asked, "Fred? As in Doctor Fred Newman?"

"Marlena set us up two months ago. Although it's unethical for a doctor to date a patient's twin sister, Marlena thought we'd make a suitable match. Why not? We were both available and had the same interests. At first, Fred was hesitant but agreed to give it a shot." A smile formed on Anita's face. "We hit it off right away."

"This is the first I heard of this."

"Fred and I wanted to keep it hush until we knew our relationship would work out. Since everything went so well, we planned on revealing the secret at this weekend's barbecue."

"You and Newman?"

"Why not? He's handsome, rich, and has the charisma women dream about." Anita placed her hand on her brother-in-law's shoulder. "I've dated my share of dirtbags, but Fred is the real deal. I held out until we visited The Do Drop Inn." She winked. "So, what brings you to Fred's office?"

THE AMBER LIGHT OF CHRISTMAS

NORTH POLE... It was late January, a month after another successful Christmas run and two weeks after the sudden death of the most famous reindeer of all. Santa called for a corporate meeting. He needed to iron out the feud between two reindeer and announce a change of command.

Santa lectured, "We can't have this, Brutus. Your behavior is unacceptable. You and Randolph need to work out your differences."

"I'll deal with him in my own way, Santa. More important is, what's the talk about a transfer of leadership all about? I've been the training commander for fifteen years. What gives?"

"Morale is at an all-time low. It's time for a change. I've received too many complaints from the herd about your Marine-like boot camp drills. You're not the most popular buck around here. I have a signed petition from every reindeer threatening to strike if you don't step down."

Brutus snorted. "My job is to train for efficiency, not make friends. I hope you're not threatening to replace me with the son of a red-nosed freak?"

"My father wasn't a freak," Randolph interrupted.

"I'm talking to Santa right now. Let's face it! A glowing red nose wasn't normal."

Randolph whined, "Make fun of him all you want, Brutus. But my father's gift made your job a heck of a lot easier."

"Stop bickering," Santa demanded. "I have enough on my plate dealing with temperamental elves and keeping tabs on who's naughty or nice. There's no time for the nonsense of feuding reindeer."

Brutus growled. "I'm telling you, Santa. Randolph lacks the personality to be a commander. His laid-back methods won't prepare the team for the big night."

"Don't make it more difficult than it is. It's time to pass the torch. Allow the younger generation to take over."

"Where does this leave me, Santa?"

"Assist Randy through the transition. Teach him the ropes. Show him the fastest routes. Give him tips on landing and takeoff procedures."

Brutus sneered at his replacement. "Let him learn himself. Nobody taught me. If he is to be the new commander, let him figure it out."

Santa lit his pipe and looked over the eyeglasses perched on his nose. "I heard the rumors. Is it true your animosity toward your replacement has nothing to do with a change of command?"

"A rumor is a circulating story with no truth behind it. It's all gossip, Santa. I would never allow my personal life to interfere with work and my responsibilities as the team commander."

"Didn't Daisy leave you? Isn't she shacking up with Randolph now?"

"That's a personal matter I'd rather not discuss. Daisy will come back to me. She always does."

"Not this time," Randolph barked. "She's tired of you flirting with every doe this side of the Arctic."

"Nobody asked you, Dud Snout. And if she doesn't come back, it's her loss."

"Knock it off, you two," yelled Santa. "Whatever the issue is between you two, work it out, and fast. If word about disgruntled reindeer leaked out to the press, it would ruin everything Christmas stands for."

Brutus raised his head and bared his teeth. "Just because Randolph is the son of a legend doesn't mean he has the leadership skills to run the sled team. Old Red Nose may have provided a guiding light through the foggy nights, but God, his navigation skills were pathetic. As far as his leadership qualities go, he couldn't lure a mouse out of a cheese factory. His useless son is no more worthy. I'm the one who held everything together. Can Randolph be the glue stick if everything falls apart? I don't think so, Santa. How can you trust him for the leadership role? If you ask my opinion, Randolph will never carry the weight of Christmas on his shoulders without crumbling. Just wait until he leads the team to the middle of nowhere and gets lost. Don't expect me to come to the rescue. I won't lift a hoof to help. I'm done." Brutus swayed his large antlers back and forth. "That's all I have to say about that."

Santa gave Brutus a long, hard stare and spoke in a calming voice. "It's time to pass the buck. I need your cooperation. Make this changeover as seamless as possible." He headed out the barn door and warned, "Come up with a peaceful solution. Bury your ego. Think of the children."

The two reindeer waited until Santa was out of hearing range before Randolph spoke. "We're on the same team, Brutus. So why pull in different directions?"

"No more charades, Randolph. We're not teammates anymore. I won't pretend to be a happy reindeer."

"You brought this on yourself, getting more controlling than ever. Because of your egotistical and self-centered attitude, the reindeer don't want to fly with you anymore."

"This is a conspiracy. The younger deer dislike me because I'm old school. The new-age reindeer are into this everyone-is-created-equal crap and believe a doe is as capable as us bucks. Dream on. Live in the real world."

"Times have changed. You refuse to adjust to the new way of thinking and have a knack for offending everyone. It was only a matter of time before an uprising. Even though I signed the petition to ask for your resignation, I never expected the herd to pick me as your successor."

Brutus stomped his hoof. "Liar. You couldn't wait to take over and impress Daisy. Are you aware of what's ahead and the responsibility that awaits you? With you at the reins, I predict disaster."

"I might surprise you."

"Christmas comes once a year. There's no margin for error. I don't want to be around when the mission fails." His nostrils flared. "If Santa wants my resignation, he'll get it. I quit. Good riddance."

"Please, Brutus. I need you on the team as my second in command."

"And I do the work, and you get the glory? No thanks." He gave Randolph a menacing stare. "Lucky for you, I respect Santa, or else I'd ram my antlers through your rib cage. But why resort to violence and risk the tabloids turning our encounter into front-page news?" Finished with his rant, Brutus stormed from the barn and galloped over the hilly horizon in search of a new habitat.

***

EARLY SPRING...

Brutus and Spice enjoyed a roll in the hay until a reindeer from the old herd showed up at the barn door. "Venus! Can't you see I'm busy?"

152

"Sorry for the interruption, Brutus, but it's important. It's Daisy. She's a mess. She needs your help."

"What's her problem now?"

"Randy's been shot. North Pole Hospital airlifted him to Greenland, where they have veterinarians who specialize in emergencies like this."

"What goes around comes around."

"Don't be so heartless. I know you and Daisy are at odds, and you've tangled antlers with Randy, but this is not the time to feud. It's bad, Brutus. Life-threatening. Daisy is beside herself. You need to be at her side to comfort her." Venus fluttered her sexy green eyes and pleaded. "Do the right thing."

"Okay, already. Gather the herd while I reach the boss on my ham radio. We'll fly down together."

***

Within hours, the herd landed in the Greenland Veterinarian Hospital parking lot and entered the main lobby. Brutus approached the cute blue-eyed arctic fox behind the receptionist's desk and asked about Randolph's condition.

"I don't have the authorization to release patient information, my deer. You will find Mrs. Randolph in the waiting pen on the second floor."

"Mrs. Randolph? There must be a mistake. Daisy and the patient never got married."

"They tied the knot a few weeks after you guys split," Venus answered. "Daisy wanted to invite you to the wedding but feared you'd cause a scene."

"Damn right, I would. It makes no sense. Randolph is a has-been who never was."

The elevator door opened as the herd assembled inside on its way to the second floor. Brutus tilted his antlers at the fluffy fox. Her purrs sent signals he had her attention.

"Don't even think about it," Venus warned. "She's too sly for you."

***

The delicate surgery to remove the bullet a hunter buried in Randolph's neck took longer than expected. During the stressful wait, Brutus refused to leave Daisy's side. Everyone scrambled to attention when an unhappy-looking security moose walked into the waiting corral. "Snowy Owl just caught a bearded, heavyset human in a red suit trying to climb down the chimney. He claims he knows the patient."

"That's Santa. He's cool," Brutus answered.

"I don't care how cool he is. This is an animal hospital. We adhere to strict regulations and allow no humans inside the premises. For health reasons. I'm sure you understand."

"No. I don't understand," Brutus barked. "How dare you discriminate against Santa because he's human? He's the face of Christmas and is as much a part of this family as any furry friend."

"Isn't it because of a human's violent nature that Randolph is fighting for his life?"

"Whoever did this, Santa will make sure his stocking is full of coal on Christmas morning."

The security moose looked down the hall. "I shouldn't do this. Chief Walrus would bite my tail off if he found out I allowed a human to enter this hospital." He peeked again to make sure no one was around. "Hurry! Sneak the old man in the crate elevator. Once he's inside the waiting pen, close the gate. Tell him to keep his mouth shut and knock off the *Ho, Ho, Ho.*"

An hour later, Doctor Wolf entered the waiting room. He ran his paws through his mane. His somber expression made the reindeer anxious.

"What's my husband's status, Doc?"

"It's too early to tell, Mrs. Randolph. The patient is stable, but there is concern about permanent neurological damage. The medical staff did all they could. All we can do now is wait."

"Suppose he can't walk or fly anymore?" Jane Doe asked. "What then?"

"Don't go there," Starbuck answered. "Randy will be fine. For the children's sake, he has to be."

"Oh please," Brutus groaned. "Don't put him on a pedestal. His father may be a folk hero and has a song written about him, but what has Randolph done besides nothing?"

Starbuck lowered his antlers and took a step closer to Brutus. "I resent you talking about our commander like that. Go home. You are no longer in charge. We don't need you around here."

Venus stepped between them. "Okay, everybody, calm down. We're all uptight with what's going on with Randy. We need to keep our heads. I'm the first to agree. Brutus can be quick with his insults, but he thrives under pressure better than any reindeer I know. We need someone to hold us together. Who else better than our former commander?"

***

While the herd paced the waiting pen, Brutus called Daisy to a quiet corner. "I noticed you've gotten chunky. What's going on? It's not like you. You've always watched your weight."

She nervously stared at her hooves. "It's nothing. It's the off-season. Too much eating and not enough exercise."

"I don't believe you. Tell me the truth."

"It's a long story. Now's not the time to get into it."

"On the contrary. This is as good a time as ever to explain. Start talking. I'm listening. I just pray you are not pregnant."

There was no sense in hiding the secret any longer. "Okay, already. I'm due in late June."

Brutus raised his head and tucked in his chin. The hair along his neck stood up straight. "How can you let this happen? I thought you were a better judge of character?"

"That's just it, Brutus. Randy is everything I could want."

"What you are saying makes no sense. Look at all those years you shacked up with me. Don't you remember the good times?"

"It's the bad times that leave a more lasting memory. Everything we did together was about you. I grew tired of you treating me like a second-class citizen because I was a female. Randy treats me as an equal."

"Okay, be that way. I hope the fawn doesn't have Randolph's daddy's red nose."

"Kind of. Extensive tests show my baby doe will have a yellow nose, which is why we are naming her Amber."

"A yellow nose? You can't make this stuff up. Aren't you embarrassed?"

"Why? I'm honored to be part of this miracle. And wouldn't it be terrific if Amber's born with the gift of flying? If Randy allows her, maybe she could eventually lead the team on Christmas Eve."

"Yeah, right? It'll be a hot day in the North Pole before a doe becomes the herd's guiding light."

"Brutus, what is your problem?"

"This is a buck's world. Females in this herd know their place. A doe is to follow, not lead."

"Back off on your bucking attitude. And stop bragging that your antlers are larger than everyone else's. Bigger doesn't mean better, and you are living proof it doesn't mean wiser."

"I didn't deserve that insult."

"It's the truth, Brutus. You are so thickheaded. Have you ever budged during an argument and admitted you were wrong?"

"When am I ever wrong?"

Daisy shook her head and mumbled, "I rest my case," before she stomped away.

"Daisy, stop. Let's talk this out."

"Let it be, Brutus. If I were you, I'd worry about Santa? Look at him sitting alone in the corner of the waiting pen. I never saw him look so down before."

Brutus pranced over to the not-so-jolly man who looked like he was contemplating deeply. "A penny for your thoughts?"

"Keep your money. You don't want to know what I'm thinking."

"Cheer up, Santa. You're talking to old Brutus here. Randolph will survive. He'll have plenty of time to recover before this winter's run."

"It's not Randolph's fate that worries me. It's a lot deeper than that."

"Deeper? As in?"

"The tradition of flying reindeer delivering presents on Christmas Eve is in great danger. The increased frequency of foggy nights on Christmas Eve will make it impossible for reindeer to navigate the skies safely. Using a sophisticated lighting system would tip off the children my sled was in the area. I weighed my alternatives. None of them I liked. I've done my darndest to avoid modern technology that would commercialize the holidays more than they already are." Santa looked around to make sure no other reindeer was listening. "Sorry, Brutus, but I've come to the crossroads and need to do whatever it takes to save Christmas."

"How long have you thought about this?"

"Eight years ago, I was about to give up and sell out when a miracle allowed me to cancel my plans."

"Are you talking about Randy's father?"

Santa nodded. "For nearly a decade, he lit the way and guided the team through the fog and darkness. Nobody expected his death two weeks after last Christmas. We will all miss his gift of light. With him gone now, I need to find an alternate way for my team to see through the fog when we deliver presents."

"What are you saying?"

"I relieved you of your duties to assure history books would not blame you for the end of the tradition of flying reindeer. I hired Randolph as your replacement, only as a morale booster for the herd. I had already decided, yet I couldn't build up my nerve to announce the massive changes in our delivery system."

"Changes? As in?"

"You've been around a long time, Brutus. The effects of global warming are causing frequent foggy nights. I won't allow the team to fly in unsafe conditions where visibility is poor. Besides that, can you imagine if we cannot meet a delivery to millions of children just once? The results would be catastrophic. Oh my, the poor children." Santa removed his glasses and wiped tears from his eyes. "I came up with a solution. It's the only way to go."

Brutus rested his front hoof on Santa's lap. "Let me hear it."

"UPS," Santa whispered.

Brutus snorted. "You're putting us out to pasture and replacing us with brown trucks?"

Santa lifted his finger to his lips. "Hush. Keep it quiet. It's a decision I regret making, but necessary if we want to avoid disappointing the children."

"When did you intend to tell everyone?"

"I was waiting for the last minute, just in case another miracle came my way."

***

The reindeer stopped reading their National Geographic magazines and gathered around when Doctor Wolf appeared.

Brutus said, "Excuse me, Santa. It's best if I'm with Daisy for this. I'll be right back."

The doctor informed Daisy of a prognosis none of the herd expected. "It's a definite game-changer, Mrs. Randolph, but our patient is fortunate he can go home in a few days. Of course, his recovery will take time. He'll need rest and relaxation, but eventually, he should be as good as new, almost."

"Explain *almost?*"

Dr. Wolf swished his tail. "Every animal knows how special it is for a reindeer to fly. There are only a few

162

dozen in the world with the ability. Most reindeer never leave the ground. I'm confident your husband will adjust to his handicap and do just fine."

"Are you saying Rudy can't fly anymore?"

"We did our best, Mrs. Randolph. But unfortunately, the bullet caused severe cartilage damage. He will never fly again, but it's a heck of a better outcome than burying him under an iceberg at the godforsaken North Pole."

Daisy wasn't sure how to feel. Randy had survived a near-death accident. He could have been much worse off. "Can I see him, Doc?"

"For just a few minutes. The patient has gone through quite an ordeal. Follow me."

Despite the unfortunate news, the atmosphere was a happy one. The bucks banged their antlers together while the does rubbed noses in celebration. Although Randolph outlived his usefulness to the sled team, he could still graze in the fields and live a productive life.

As the herd celebrated, Brutus returned to his boss to continue their discussion. "Santa. The miracle you prayed for is on its way."

"What miracle?"

"Amber."

"Who is Amber?"

"Daisy is pregnant with Randolph's fawn. Her little one will have a glowing nose, just like her grandfather, except hers will be yellow, maybe even brighter than a red nose. With baby Amber lighting the sky, she can keep the tradition alive."

"That sounds fine and dandy, but the odds of her being a flying reindeer are slim to none. Even if she has a glowing nose, what good is it if she can't fly?"

"Daisy is due in June. So, we should know by early December if Baby Amber is an aviation reindeer or not."

"That doesn't give us much time. The Farmers' Almanac predicts a cold and damp winter with many foggy nights."

"Don't worry, Santa. Keep the brown trucks in the garage. I've got this covered. I'll strap Amber on my back for our Christmas Eve run. She won't have to fly."

"A female lead? Anyone but you, Brutus. Why the change of heart?"

"Randolph said it best. A good leader needs to adjust to the times. We are all part of the same team. It shouldn't matter if a doe or buck leads the way. What's important is the children receive their presents. It's about the kids, Santa. It's all about the kids."

Santa's belly shook like Jell-O. Thanks to Amber, the light of Christmas will continue to glow.

AMANDA'S SEDUCTION

"Check it out, Tommy," Paul said as he pointed toward the attractive, middle-aged woman with the low-cut dress sitting alone at the bar. "Isn't that Melissa's mom?"

"You're right, Paul, but what the hell is she wearing?"

Paul nodded in approval. "She was a fox when you dated Melissa in high school. And shit, man, she's still got it. Christ, she's a senior citizen. Look at her. Wow!"

"I don't like what I see."

"What's not to like? She's gorgeous. It's no secret where Melissa got her looks from."

Seeing the seductively dressed Mrs. Harper alone on a barstool concerned me. I'd known her since I was a teenager. Her revealing dress was out of character, and I noticed Mr. Harper wasn't with her. I wondered if everything was okay. I walked over to say hello. Our eyes met. She offered a blank stare before a smile of recognition. "I don't believe it. Tommy McGraw. You're looking great."

"I'm doing what I can to stay in shape. How are you and Mr. Harper?"

She held out her left hand, absent a wedding ring. "We divorced years ago."

"I'm so sorry."

She shrugged her shoulders. "Don't blame Jim. It was my fault. But hey, there's no reason to depress you with a boring account of the rise and fall of Amanda Harper. Let's change subjects. What's going on in your life? Hope you've made better choices than me."

"Have a wife and two kids at home. We've hit an occasional rough patch along the way, but we're still together."

"Last I heard, you moved to Texas. What brings you back to your old neighborhood?"

"The high school reunion is tomorrow night. Thirty years. Do you believe it? Paul and I were reminiscing about our wild teenage days. I hope Melissa stops by to say hello. She graduated three years after me, but I'd love to see her again."

She squeezed my hands tight. "You're even better looking than when my daughter introduced you to the family back in tenth grade. Jim and I were positive you two would tie the knot."

"I think of Melissa often. How's she doing?"

"She left home twenty years ago. Told me to go to hell. I haven't heard from her since."

Ouch! Rather than pry and ask questions, I embraced her. She clung to me with all her might.

"Are you okay, Mrs. Harper?"

"No, I'm not. My life sucks. But I won't burden you with the dark clouds hovering over my head." She took a sip of her martini. "I made my bed. Now I'll die in it."

"I don't like what I'm hearing."

"Then go join Paul and continue talking about your wild teenage days."

"Mrs. Harper. Your divorce, the conflict with Melissa, the way you're dressed, is so unlike you."

"It's my problem, not yours."

"I'm a good listener. Care to talk?"

She looked around the crowded bar. "How about saving me cab fare? Drive me to my apartment. We'll discuss this further in private."

"You have no car?"

"I lost my license after my third DWI."

"Mrs. Harper? I always looked up to you. How can you be so reckless? What is going on in your life?"

168

"If you're interested, then why not drive me home? I'll give you an earful."

"It's not that I'm interested, as much as I feel you need someone to talk to."

I jiggled my car keys to catch Paul's attention and signaled I was going to Mrs. Harper's place. He gave him the thumbs-up sign. He had the wrong idea. I reminded myself to call him tomorrow with the disappointing news I didn't pop the old lady.

Moments after we entered her apartment, she wrapped her arms around my neck and pressed her lips against mine. I pushed her away and chose my words carefully, making it clear I had no plans to jump into the sack with an ex-girlfriend's mother. "I understand how empty your heart must be, Mrs. Harper, and you have serious issues you need to address. If you wish to talk, I'm here to listen. Whatever you say will remain between us. It's our secret. Okay!"

She apologized, agreeing her actions were wrong, confessing she was going through rough times and needed a shoulder to cry on. Rather than make a big deal over it, we got down to why she invited me to her apartment.

"It began in the summer of '69," she began. "Fifteen and pregnant. My family, fed up with my carefree lifestyle, disowned me, leaving me alone with the tough decision about what to do with the unwanted baby."

"Does Melissa know she has a brother?"

"Not even Jim, the man who fathered Melissa three years later, is aware I gave birth to another child. The only other person who knows this is my shrink." She continued to recount her journey, with honesty, as she detailed every wrong turn and dead-end along her bumpy road.

"I don't know what to say, Mrs. Harper."

"Say nothing, Tommy. I'm no saint, and I've had countless affairs during my marriage. One afternoon, Melissa came home early from work and caught me in bed with her fiancé. The marriage was off, Melissa moved away, and Mr. Harper filed for divorce."

Wanting to scold her, I thought better of it. These secrets were tearing at her insides. She needed someone to listen without asking questions.

"I hid my pain and loneliness with alcohol, cocaine, and more bed partners than I remember." She wiped her tears before pleading, "Please hold me."

What happened next wasn't on my to-do list. Mrs. Harper had her own ideas the moment she invited me to her apartment. When the morning sun peeked through the bedroom window, my thoughts were of Melissa. How would she react if she knew what her mother and ex-boyfriend were up to? Sleeping with a woman seventeen years my senior was insane, even if she had the stamina and body of someone half her age.

Another one-nighter for Mrs. Harper. I hope she understood why it couldn't be anything more. Although she was the aggressor, I felt guilty about allowing it to go as far as it did. It shouldn't have happened.

When she lit a cigarette, I climbed out of bed to look closer at the magnificent portrait of Melissa hanging on the wall. Just below the picture was a framed Woodstock ticket. "My mother attended Woodstock too."

"So did four hundred thousand other people. Woodstock was an event of a lifetime and the reason for the emptiness in my heart." She climbed out of bed and walked over to the portrait. She placed her hand on the ticket. "I bought this at a collectible show. It's the only link to my son. He has the original ticket."

"Son? Melissa has a brother?"

"I had him out of wedlock. Before I met Jim."

Chills ran down my spine. "Why does your son have the original ticket?"

"It's a long story."

"Before we go any further, meet me in the kitchen after you put clothes on. I picked my garments off the floor and carried them into the bathroom to dress and splash cold water on my face.

A minute later, she appeared in a sexy robe with the belt dangling at her side. "Please, Mrs. Harper. Cover up."

"What's with the sudden modesty? Last night, you couldn't keep your hands off me. I heard no complaints when I taught you positions you never knew existed. Now, you avoid me. Do I look that bad in the daylight?"

"I'm just second-guessing what took place last night."

"Don't freak out. I don't expect a commitment."

"It could be more complicated than that, Mrs. Harper."

"Stop the Mrs. Harper crap. It's Amanda." She slid the robe off her shoulders. "You got to admit, Tommy. I'm hot for a woman my age."

"Please cover yourself and answer my questions with honest answers."

"I don't need clothes on to talk." She stood before me in her birthday suit. "Make it quick. The bedroom is waiting."

"We may not have that desire afterward." I did my best not to focus on places I shouldn't and began my questioning. "What became of Melissa's brother?"

"I did what was necessary."

"Which means?"

"I've been more honest with you than I have with my shrink. I've told you more than enough."

"What does Woodstock have to do with this?"

"It was a wild weekend. I never thought to get last names or telephone numbers." She took a long drag of her cigarette. "It took two missing periods before I realized I was pregnant."

"How many were there?"

"I wasn't counting. The Woodstock Festival was a crowded place. I don't need a lecture from you. It happened a long time ago. The past is the past. Give it a rest."

"Did you put the baby up for adoption?"

"Next question."

"Answer me, dammit!"

"It's none of your business."

"It could be," I shouted as I ripped the cigarette from her lips.

Her eyes grew cloudy. "I'm not sure why you need to know, but an anonymous wealthy couple offered me the financial security to go through with the pregnancy. I saw dollar signs. There were no third-party or adoption agencies, no records to trace, or fear of the kid disrupting my life years later. Just how I wanted it. The money helped get my feet on the ground, and my son was certain of a good home."

"What if your son stood in front of you? Would you know who he is?"

"No, I wouldn't, and it haunts me, especially with my life crumbling the way it has. I gave birth to two children and have no contact with either. I'd give anything to have him in my life, but he doesn't know I exist. The only link between us is the concert ticket I initialed M.E. for Mandy Evans and tucked inside his blanket minutes after birth. Who was I kidding? His parents surely destroyed the ticket as soon as they discovered it."

Her words ripped my insides apart. It felt like someone kicked me in the balls. My hands trembled as I laid a laminated Woodstock ticket on the counter. "I've carried this memento in my wallet since I was old enough to understand. It belonged to my birth mom. Only a handful of people know I'm not the biological child of the McGraw's."

She stared at the ticket and turned it over to see her faded initials. She reached for her robe to cover her body.

"Oh, my God, Tommy! What have we done?"

FIRE IN HIS HEART

"Hell of a blaze, men. Drinks are on the house."

A loud cheer came from a dozen exhausted firefighters who stopped in for a beer or three filled the room.

Gabe, the bartender, set beers in front of Cliff and Luke. "Any fatalities?"

Luke nodded. "A few. We did our best. It's not every day a plane crashes into an apartment building."

"It's scary when it happens down the block," Gabe said. He then turned his attention to a group of firefighters at the other end of the bar.

Working on his second beer, Cliff scolded his buddy, "What were you thinking, Luke? Nobody in their right mind enters a towering inferno. Just when I thought you were toast, I see you climbing down a ladder surrounded in flames with a puppy tucked under your arm. Are you crazy?"

"I couldn't leave the little guy locked in his crate to burn to death."

"It's a dog, for Christ's sake. Next time don't be suicidal."

"Hey! Somebody in that apartment loved their pooch. Whether an animal or a person doesn't matter. It's still a living creature."

"So is a cockroach. Firefighters put out fires and risk their lives to rescue people, not a freakin' mutt."

"Let it be, Cliff." Luke stood. "Hold the stool for me while I hit the men's room."

A tall, slender, attractive young woman with waist-long red hair, wearing a soiled T-shirt with the words, *It's Five O'clock Somewhere,* approached Cliff. "Excuse me, sir. Is the hero firefighter who endangered his life to rescue my friend's dog here? The Fire Captain said his name is Luke."

"You're in luck, pretty lady. The empty barstool belongs to the one you're looking for. He'll be right back."

When Luke returned, the woman wrapped her arms around him and planted her lips on his. "Maureen can't be here to thank you, so I'm doing it for her."

"What did I do to deserve the honor of a beautiful woman embracing me?"

"You saved Patches from a horrible death."

"Patches?"

"My roommate's dog."

"Please don't put me on a pedestal. It's what firefighters do."

"If that's the case, why were you the only firefighter to enter the blaze to save the animal?" She took his hand and led him toward the exit. "We need to talk. In private."

As they left O'Malley's, a handful of firefighters gave the thumbs-up sign. Another called out, "Go for it, Luke."

"My name's McKenzie. My roommate and I were having breakfast in the cafeteria when the fire broke out. Instead of leaving the building, Maureen headed back to her room on the third floor to get her dog. I watched in horror as the stairwell collapsed, burying her under a pile of burning debris, killing her instantly."

"Jeez, I'm so sorry."

McKenzie nodded her head. Tears ran down her face. "Words can't express my sorrow. My best friend is dead, I'm homeless, and everything I owned is in ashes."

"Anything I can do?"

"You've already done more than enough. But a lift to the animal shelter to pick up Patches and a quick stop at the pet store will really help. He needs food, a leash, and a tennis ball."

"No problem. I'll do whatever I can."

"How about a place to crash tonight?"

"The Holiday Inn has reasonable rates."

"Won't work. No animals allowed." She gazed at him with her large, expressive green eyes. "Please don't think this is a come-on, but would you object if I spend the night with you?"

"My tiny apartment has one bed."

"One bed is all we need."

After finishing the errands, the exhausted couple hit the sack. Unfortunately, they got little sleep or anything else with the dog lying between their feet. Licks to the face woke Luke the following morning.

McKenzie had left, leaving behind a note on the nightstand.

Dear Luke,

Wish we had met under happier circumstances. Sorry for splitting without saying goodbye, but I'm close with Maureen's mom. My place is to be with her to help with funeral arrangements. She's a lovely lady, but not an animal lover. She'll be bitter when she learns her daughter lost her life trying to save the dog. I hate to put you on the spot, but it's best if you puppy-sit until after the burial. Hope it won't be a bother.

Let's meet at the cemetery, a week from Sunday, to give Patches one last chance to be with her. I punched the address into your GPS. Someone in the office will tell you where to find her. I'll be waiting for you.

BTW: My lifestyle makes it impossible to care for an animal. Would owning a dog fit into your plans? He's a good boy. You're a good man. I'm confident you'll give him the loving home he deserves. Think about it.

Until we meet again,
Love ya both.
McKenzie

"No way," Luke grunted as he heaved the tennis ball across the room. Patches retrieved it, dropped it at his feet, and stared at him with sad eyes. It's unfair to take my frustrations out on the dog, so I rubbed him behind his ears. "It's okay, boy. McKenzie will figure something out." He then mumbled, "This won't work. I have no time for a dog."

A week from Sunday, Luke drove to New Jersey with Patches in the backseat. The GPS took him to Holy Cross Cemetery. He parked his car and opened the backdoor to attach the dog's leash. Patches darted from his grasp and sped across the cemetery. Luke chased after him. The hyper puppy stopped to lie on top of a newly dug grave. An elderly woman looked on in bewilderment.

"I'm sorry," Luke said. "This isn't my dog. Patches belonged to a woman who died in a recent fire. I've been watching him for the deceased woman's girlfriend."

The woman broke down crying. "That stupid mutt is the reason my daughter is dead. I don't want it anywhere near Maureen."

"My deepest condolences for your loss, but please don't take it out on the dog. Your daughter loved him so much."

"I've come here every day since her burial, sitting here for hours. Since she moved out of the house after college, I don't know much about her friends. How well did you know Maureen?"

"I never met her, but I met her roommate. I'm returning the dog to her today. Wonder why she's late."

"My daughter had no roommate. What was her name?"

"McKenzie. Sorry, she never gave me her last name."

"Never heard of her."

"That's strange! From the way she spoke, you two were tight."

"What did she look like?"

"An attractive redhead in her mid-twenties. Eyes greener than Ireland."

The woman gasped and placed her hands over her mouth. "My daughter's full name was Maureen

McKenzie. Your friend fits my daughter's description. Was she tall and thin, five-nine with waist-long hair?"

Chills went through Luke's body. Maureen and McKenzie are the same people. There was no reason to upset her mother more than she already was. I lied. "Just the opposite. McKenzie was short and stocky, with hair not much longer than mine."

Patches carried his leash over to Luke, hinting it was time to leave. McKenzie wasn't coming to greet them. She was already here, six feet below. "Gotta go, Mrs. McKenzie. Looks like she stood me up, but I understand. Until we meet again, I'll take good care of Patches." Luke tugged on Patches' leash. "Let's go home, boy. It's just you and me now."

VENDETTA

Johnny Bianco, a big player in the Frankie Randazzo Crime Family, worked on the south side of Chicago. Known as Johnny B. Bad, he dirtied his hands in drugs, firearms, prostitution, gambling, and an occasional strong-arm when someone stepped out of line. Many nights he came home with an unfortunate victim's blood on his clothing. Other nights, the smell of a woman's perfume. When his wife Maria questioned his whereabouts and activities, she learned the hard way to keep her mouth shut and eyes closed. Trapped in an abusive marriage with a cheating husband, her only way out would be inside a coffin.

One afternoon, Maria returned home from food shopping and did not like what she saw. Her husband and Sal Randazzo, Frankie's wise ass son were sitting in the den drinking beer. Unhappy with the gangster in her home, she told her daughter to play in her room and went into the kitchen to put away the groceries.

When she finished, Johnny called out to her. "Come in here. Sal needs a favor from you."

Maria mumbled under her breath, "I wouldn't give this punk the time of day, and he wants a favor? Fat chance of that happening."

She walked into the den. Johnny spoke.

"The headline dancer at Randazzo's nightclub overdosed last night. Sal is in a bind and is asking if you could volunteer your services until he finds a replacement. The pay is good."

"Volunteer what services?"

"Everyone knows what a fabulous dancer you are."

"Get to the point, Johnny. What does Sal want me to do?"

"You know what women dancers do at Randazzo's. With your equipment, you'd be a natural."

"I'll never stoop so low."

"Excuse me, Sal. Give me a minute to talk sense into my wife."

He motioned her to join him in the kitchen.

"Listen to me. The Randazzo's have narrowed the competition for the vacated territory between Stretch Costanza and me." He held his thumb and forefinger an inch apart. "I am this close. Returning this favor would seal the deal. Do it for me. For us."

"Are you crazy? You can't expect me to strut my stuff in front of a room full of horny perverts."

"You're my wife and you do as I say. It's not your choice. I risk my life in the streets and give you luxuries you only dreamed of before you met me. I've busted my ass for years. You have no say in the matter."

She walked over to the door, opened it, and motioned for Sal to leave. "You're not welcome in my home, Randazzo. Don't come back."

Furious, Johnny jumped from the couch and slapped her across her face. "What the hell is wrong with you? Sal's father is our lifeline. Without him, we got nothing."

Maria felt blood running from her nostril as it had so many times before when Johnny expressed his anger.

"If you continue to give me a hard time, you'll have more than a nosebleed to worry about. When I tell you to do something, you do it."

"Don't I have a say in this? It's my body."

"You've had a free ride since we married. It's time you earn your keep."

"If you're looking for a stripper, why not try asking one of your girlfriends?"

"What's the big deal? They're strangers. They don't know you. You don't know them."

"When I married you, I didn't sign up for this."

Sal interrupted. "All I want is a yes or no. I don't have all day here. If your fuckin wife isn't interested, there is always Angel Constanza. She's a hot broad too, but her tits aren't as big as Maria's. Last call! If your wife doesn't get her head out of her ass, Angel will work out just fine."

"Dammit, Maria. Help me out here."

"What you expect of me is so humiliating."

"In this business, we've all done shit we didn't want to do. We do it anyway because the situation calls for it. This is one of those times you need to do whatever is necessary."

"No way!"

"There better be a way, sweetheart," Sal interrupted. "If not, your husband can kiss the new territory goodbye. It's a shame too. It's a golden opportunity for Frankie that would move him up the chain in the Randazzo Syndicate. And he's gonna miss out because his stuck-up wife won't take her clothes off on stage. I told you the money was good."

"This is not about the almighty dollar, Sal. We are doing well financially. I'm happy in the place I'm at. Now get the hell out of here?"

Johnny pinned her against the wall and wrapped his huge right hand around her throat. He released his grip ten seconds later. She collapsed to the floor, gasping for air. He raised his foot as if to kick her.

"Do what I say, or I'll give you a beating like you never had before. Get your ass up! Tell Sal you will gladly be the clubs entertainment until he finds a replacement."

Maria struggled to her feet and remained silent.

"She'll come around, Sal. By showtime, she'll be ready to give your audience a show they'll never forget."

"I knew your bitch wife would come around. They always do. But before we make it official, I need an audition for the job. You know? To make sure there are no surprises, and everything is in the right place."

"Trust me, Sal. Everything is where it's supposed to be."

Maria wiped her bleeding nose with the back of her hand. "It doesn't matter what I have or where it is. Sal or nobody else at the club will ever see it."

"Get your ass up and show Sal how talented you are."

Maria finally came around. Tears poured from her eyes. "Okay. Okay. Whatever you want, Johnny. I'll do it. Just please, give me a few minutes to stop my nose bleed."

Johnny kissed his wife on the forehead. "You're the best. I knew you'd come through."

She headed toward the master bath. "When I'm ready, all I ask is we do this in the bedroom, so our daughter doesn't see what's going on."

"Five minutes," Sal said. "Not a minute more."

"Don't rush me, Salvador. I'm worth the wait."

Eight minutes later, the impatient Sal called out, "What's the delay?"

"I don't want to do this, men. There must be another way."

"You have no choice. You've stalled long enough. We're coming in, ready or not. Let the entertainment begin."

The two gangsters charged into the bedroom and stopped in their tracks. Maria held a shotgun in her arms. "Enjoy the show."

"What the..."

Sal never finished his sentence. Her first shot splattered his blood and brains against the wall. A second blast, aimed three feet lower, left Johnny without his pride and joy and not much else below the waist.

Maria called out to her daughter. "Stay in your room, honey. Mommy will come to get you in a few minutes."

Maria packed two suitcases, emptied the cash from the dead men's wallets, grabbed the storage box full of cash, and sped off with her daughter in her Jaguar. She crossed the Indiana state line to make it appear she was heading eastbound before ditching the car and hailing a cab to the nearest Greyhound Terminal. She headed toward California to hook up with a former Randazzo associate. Tony Greco would help Maria Bianco disappear.

GUILTY

Chapter 1
Twenty-six years ago,
1993

Roger and Linda Brinkman struggled to stay together for their daughter's sake. They hurdled the obstacles in their path, determined to make the marriage work. But the suspicion of his wife's affair was one roadblock Roger couldn't overcome. They argued. She denied any wrongdoing, although the signs were obvious. Unwilling to ignore her lies anymore, Roger's voice grew louder. Their four-year-old daughter stood in the doorway hugging her stuffed animal.

"Look what you did, asshole," Linda hollered. "With you carrying on like a lunatic, you woke Madison from her nap."

"I have reason to rant and rave. My wife is screwing around."

The child began crying. Roger grabbed his car keys and bent down on his knees to hug his distraught daughter. "It's okay, honey. Daddy will be back in a few days. Be a good girl while I'm away."

"Where the hell do you think you're going?" Linda yelled.

"To get away from you and clear my head. When you're ready to admit what you've been up to, you know where to reach me."

He stormed out of the house. Linda followed, giving him the middle finger as he backed out of the driveway.

***

Fueled by rage, Roger's usual hour-and-a-half drive took him only seventy-five minutes. Once inside the beach house, he dropped onto the loveseat and tried to think. How could Linda do this to him? He tolerated enough of her crap through the years, now a complete betrayal.

He thought of his options. A divorce would have a lasting psychological effect on little Madison. Forgiveness? Never happen. She crossed over the forbidden line. He couldn't look the other way anymore. Not this time.

Unable to focus, he called his best friend to run it by him. Danny knew Linda's idiosyncrasies better than anyone.

Danny answered on the third ring.

"It's Roger. We need to talk. It's about Linda. You have a few minutes?"

"I always have time for my friends. What's wrong? From the tone in your voice, it sounds serious."

After listening to Roger rant for five minutes, Danny pleaded, "Enough already. You're locked in gear. It's unlike you to be so bent out of shape. You guys are my closest friends. The best I can do is keep an open mind about this. There are two sides to every story. I shouldn't make judgments about your suspicions until I hear Linda's side. Give it a day to work itself out. Knowing Linda like I do, there must be a logical explanation. I'm positive your suspicions are off-base. She would never drift."

"Then why be so defensive when I confronted her?"

"How would you react if someone accused you of something you didn't do?"

"There is enough proof, Danny. It's not my imagination. I put up with her lies, jealousy, and temper tantrums for a long time. Now, this? How can I forgive her?"

"Things are not always as they seem, so before you hire a divorce lawyer, think of Madison. She needs both parents."

"And do what? Sleep on the couch while Linda shares our bed with her boyfriend?"

"Don't blow this out of proportion. Your head is not clear. You can use a distraction right about now. Hibernating like a recluse, thinking gloom and doom will only make it worse. You need to talk this out with someone. How about I pick up a six-pack and a pizza and stop down by you?"

"Alcohol won't clear my head. And I have no appetite. Besides, I've been on the phone with you for a half-hour, and I sense you taking Linda's side. I don't need you telling me to look the other way. This is serious shit."

"Okay, Rog. Suppose I send over Gail. She can give you a female perspective on her read on this."

"The fewer people who know about Linda's antics, the better. I'll ride this one out alone."

At seven o'clock, Roger heard a knock on the door. *Dammit! I hope that's not Danny.* "Who is it?"

A female voice answered, "Pizza delivery."

"Wrong address, lady," Roger called out without leaving the loveseat. "I didn't order a pizza."

"Curtesy of Daniel Jovino. He said you'll think better with a full stomach. It's already paid for."

"Jesus Christ," he grunted as he stood up and walked to the door. On the front steps stood the mother of his daughter's playmate, holding a pizza and a bottle of wine. "Gail. What are you doing here?"

"Danny sent me. I hear you're going through a difficult time right now. He's worried about you. So am I. He thought it might be a good idea if I drove over and did what I could to soften the pain. Maybe I can give some helpful advice."

"Danny has a big mouth. He knew I wanted to be alone. I can't believe he sent you all the way out here."

"I came voluntarily because I care. Besides, it's the least I can do after you saved my daughter's life last week. If you want me to leave, I understand."

"No, it's okay. You drove a long way. Come inside. There is enough pizza and wine for both of us."

Hesitant to discuss the situation, because Linda and Gail saw each other every day with their daughters, Roger explained, "It's a personal problem. I don't know you well enough to go into details."

"Danny told me what's going on. I know where you are coming from. I also had a bad marriage and kept what went on behind closed doors private. Until I couldn't take it anymore. I just hope you and Linda don't go down the same road I went with my ex-husband. It's not pretty."

"I'm trying to avoid taking that route and seeing Madison caught in the crossfire. She's the one who'd get hurt the most."

"She's a sweet girl, Roger. So pleasant and well-behaved. It's wonderful how well Madison and Jess play together. These kids have a bond like I've never seen in children so young. But Linda? There is something about her I don't trust. Can't put my finger on it, but ... let me say this. You deserve better."

The pizza filled his hunger. The wine relaxed his nerves. With three slices remaining in the box, she suggested he save room for dessert.

"I'm full. Can't eat another bite."

She leaned over and wrapped her arms around his neck. "What if I told you I'm the dessert?"

On the other side of town

"This can't continue, Linda," her best friend Tanya warned as they drove to Danny's house. "You guys have a young daughter who loves you both equally. Don't throw away your marriage over an affair that'll go nowhere. Been there, done that with three ex-husbands. End this infatuation before Roger serves you with divorce papers. It's not worth the tradeoff."

A minute later, Linda pulled her SUV in front of Danny's house and turned off the engine. "What you're saying makes perfect sense, but Danny is a great lover, and makes me feel like a woman, if you know what I mean."

"I hear you, girlfriend. But Danny is not the type to settle down. He'll promise you the world today and break your heart tomorrow. He's not worth throwing away all you have."

"He told me last week, his roaming days are behind him and he's ready to settle down."

"Do you believe in the tooth fairy too? Dammit, girl, open your eyes. He's using you the same way he uses all his women. And if you believe he isn't doing his gorgeous tenant, think again."

"You think so?"

"Duh! Gail lives under the same roof as him. He's always watching her kid when she goes out for a few hours. I'm sure he's getting something in return."

"You're right. I have too much to lose. Even if he is a great lover."

Tanya winked, "We both know that, don't we?"

"Whoa, slow down! You and Danny? When?"

"We'll talk about it when we hit Starbucks after you say goodbye to Mr. Studmeister." Tanya pointed to Danny's house. "Dump him! Now! I'll wait in the car. And don't give him a chance to coax you into one for the road."

With a half-grin, Linda joked, "You've worn out three husbands. You giving advice is like Ray Charles being Stevie Wonder's seeing-eye dog."

"Do as I say, not as I do."

Linda gave her best friend a worried look. "Do you think I can save my marriage?"

"Ditching Romeo is a step in the wright direction. Now, go do it! You have ten minutes. Any longer, I'm coming to get you."

***

Roger woke early the following morning to find Gail wasn't lying next to him. He jumped out of bed. Her car was not in the driveway. She had left during the night, leaving behind only memories of a passionate evening that only complicated his problems at home. Two wrongs didn't make a right. Ready to divorce his wife over an affair, he did the same damn thing.

If their marriage had any chance of surviving, they needed counseling. He called and left a message on the answering machine, telling Linda he'd be home in less than two hours and to drop Madison off at a sitter.

Roger never arrived home that afternoon. Two state troopers pulled over his Mercedes on the San Diego Freeway and ordered him to open his trunk. When he did, he dropped to his knees and cried out, "Oh my god. No! No! No!"

San Diego Courtroom

Despite the air-conditioning, sweat beaded on Roger's forehead. A dozen solemn men and women filed into the courtroom and sat in the jurors' box.

Judge Copperfield asked, "Has the jury reached a verdict?"

The jury foreman stood. "Yes, Your Honor."

Roger prayed God would have his back. He thought about the in-laws getting custody of his young daughter. But it wouldn't happen. He'd walk out of the courtroom a free man. Despite the tragedy, he and Madison would rebuild their lives.

The spectators waited in silence as the jury foreman handed the verdict slip to the bailiff, who passed it to the stone-faced judge.

The jury foreman cleared his throat. "We, the jurors empaneled in the case of the State of California versus Roger Brinkman, find the defendant guilty on two charges of Murder in the First Degree."

Chapter 2

San Pelican Bay State Prison--- 2019

"Brinkman, you have a visitor," said correctional officer Zack Robinson. "Some lady detective wants to run a few questions by you."

"If it has anything to do with Manny's stabbing, I already told you guys, I didn't see shit."

"Don't complain, man. The babe is a gorgeous, well-put-together strawberry blonde."

Brinkman held the latest David Baldacci novel in the air. "I can't put this book down. Tell the Barbie Doll cop to reschedule. I'm busy."

Zack snatched the book from the prisoner. "She's on a tight schedule. Let's not keep her waiting."

Roger reluctantly followed Zack to the interrogation room. He grumbled at the woman, who looked more like a glamorous movie star than a cop. "What's so damn important?"

"Please take a seat, Mr. Brinkman." She flashed her badge. "Detective Sadler, Delray Beach Homicide, on special assignment with the San Diego Police Department. I have questions about your wife's murder."

"After twenty-six years? What's the hurry?"

Sadler stared him down. "You've wasted away half your life for crimes you claim you didn't commit. If you are innocent and tired of living in this hellhole, then welcome my visit."

"Yeah, right? Like it'll make a difference?"

"Don't underestimate me. I didn't become the youngest woman in the history of the Delray Beach PD to make Detective Sergeant for no reason."

"I know the game. With the looks of a supermodel, it's easy to open doors and climb the ladder of success. If you weren't as hot as you are, you'd be directing church traffic."

Sadler leaned across the table and put her face only inches from his. "Don't bite the hand that feeds you."

"If that hand feeds me poison, I will. Excuse me for my lack of faith in the legal system, but it sucks. I had a terrible judge, an even worse attorney, a friend who turned his back on me, and an alibi who disappeared.

Not to mention a brain-dead jury and a daughter who disowned me."

"We can't change the past. Let's work together to fix the future. I'm in your corner. Give me a chance to help. You need to take me seriously."

"Can I?"

"You should. I'm your only hope."

"Do you believe I'm innocent?"

She shrugged. "On paper, you appear guilty as hell. The evidence points your way."

"If I'm guilty, why are you here?"

"Life isn't paper. Convince me you're innocent. Tell me the truth about what went on that night? If you are honest with me, maybe, just maybe, I can help you get out of this place."

"Fat chance of that happening. And how is the Delray PD involved with a crime in California?"

"I'm the one asking the questions, so let's cut to the chase. Is it true your marriage was hanging by a thread?"

"We had nothing in common anymore. If not for our daughter, we wouldn't have stayed together as long as we did."

"What's this about the argument your neighbors heard on the morning before your wife's death?"

Roger's knee-jerking shook the table. "You know damn well. Everyone in the courtroom learned of my suspicions that Linda was having an affair."

"Were your suspicions warranted?"

Roger sighed. "You tell me, Detective? Linda couldn't explain the condom and matchbook cover with the logo of a local motel I found in her pocketbook. Or the hickey she had on the side of her neck her turtleneck sweater couldn't hide. We hadn't had a special occasion in years. I sure as hell had reason to confront her."

"Confront her, yes. Killing her was an extreme measure."

"I didn't kill anyone."

"Twelve jurors thought otherwise."

"Twelve jurors were wrong. Because of their carelessness, I've wasted my best years locked inside a cage the size of a walk-in closet, deprived of watching my daughter grow up. Madison is thirty years old. Is she married? Do I have grandkids? Does she care if I'm dead or alive?"

"Maybe someday you can ask her those questions in person. But first, we need to prove your innocence and get you out of this place."

"An unlikely scenario."

"Who knows? Perhaps your horror story will have a happy ending."

"Yeah, right?"

She clapped her hands together. "We're drifting off course here. Let's get back to business. Tell me about your alibi?"

"Gail was a private person who rented a basement apartment from my friend Danny for eight months. Our daughters played together. My wife knew her better than I did. And yes, Detective, before you ask me, Ms. Vaughn was quite a looker."

"According to the police, the woman who claimed to be Gail Vaughn died two years before you met her."

"Gail was no ghost. She was very much alive."

Sadler laughed. "I'm sure she was. But who was this woman? Why was she using a dead person's identity?"

"I wouldn't know. Aside from that one night, we never had a one-on-one conversation."

"Wasn't she friends with your wife?"

"They saw each other because their daughters played together. But they weren't close."

"Is it true you saved Gail's daughter's life?"

"What does that have to do with anything?"

"Maybe nothing. Maybe everything. Tell me about it."

"A week before the murders, Danny invited me, Linda, Tanya, and Gail to join him on his new boat. Madison and Gail's daughter tagged along. Danny adored kids and treated Jessica as if she was his own daughter. He spoiled her with occasional trips to Baskin-Robbins and volunteered to babysit whenever Gail had something on her schedule."

"Let's get back to you saving Jessica's life."

"We were out in the Pacific and got careless. We weren't watching the kids as close as we should have. Jessica fell overboard in an area populated by sharks. I dove in and got her back onboard before the sharks got aggressive."

"A brave act, Mr. Brinkman."

"Jess wasn't breathing. Her lips turned blue. I did CPR, mouth to mouth, and chest compressions until she spit up water. Thank God I got her heart beating again. When we returned to shore, Danny drove Gail and Jessica to the hospital to make sure the kid checked out okay." Roger shrugged his shoulders. "With all the confusion, Gail never thanked me until she delivered more than a pizza."

Sadler showed a hint of a smile. "Tell me about Tanya Thompson?"

"A close friend of Linda's." He cuffed his hands six inches from his chest to describe her well-endowment. "Divorced a few times. I'd rather not speak ill of the dead, but she had a reputation."

"Danny testified how Tanya confided in him about her long-going affair with her best friend's husband."

"That was bullshit. The judge overruled my attorney's objection. When it came time for cross-examination, my attorney did a piss-poor job."

"Why would Tanya tell him this?"

"Who the hell knows? I never touched her. Nobody believed me. Do you know Danny popped her a few times? He once showed me a bunch of compromising Polaroids he took of her."

"And you had no interest in following Danny's lead?"

"I'm a guy. Tanya was a complete package. I'd be lying if I said I didn't fantasize about her. But that's as far as it went. Fantasizing. Even if I were a player, it would be suicidal hooking up with my wife's best friend."

"Not even in a weak moment?"

"Go to hell, Detective. A jury already convicted me. I don't need some hot-shot cop who was still in her diapers when the murders took place to question my integrity. And you know what? I figured you out. You came here to get a confession. The courts want to close the books on Roger Brinkman. You are wasting your time. I'm not confessing to anything, because I'm innocent." He called out to Zack. "Take me to my cell. I have a book to read."

"You're not going anywhere, Mr. Brinkman. We'll stay in this room all night if we must."

"You can't force me. I may be a prisoner, but I have my rights. Zack! Get the warden in here."

"You have a strange way of treating your friends."

"We are not friends. Far from it. If it weren't for your fabulous looks, I wouldn't even want to set eyes on you. As stunning as you are, I see you as an ugly person"

"This is the first time anybody called me ugly, but I have thick skin. I can handle anything you throw at me.

It's a shame you can't. I recommend you be more accommodating. You're only hurting yourself. Answer my questions." She folded her arms across her chest. "For what it's worth, I'm not looking for a confession."

"I'm not listening anymore. I'm done. My ears are closed."

"I'll talk louder. You'll hear me. Stop pouting. Put your big boy pants on. Be thankful for a second chance."

"Knock off the charades. I'll never see the outside of this shithole. Save the taxpayers' money. You can't do shit for me."

"Don't give up. A reliable source stepped forward with information that could be a game-changer."

"What information?"

"I'm still checking it out. Meanwhile, stop fighting me. Explain the large bra the same size Tanya wore under your pillow, her necklace on the floor, and the dark hair particles on the sheets? Linda and Gail were blondes."

"I can't. I washed the bedding before I left."

"Coroner's office estimated the two women's time of death somewhere between seven pm and midnight. The same hours you claim Gail was with you. If your *get out of jail free card* hadn't split, she could have been your alibi." Sadler placed her elbows on the table and rested her chin in her hands, "Correct me if I'm wrong. You fight with your wife over her affair. Then jump in bed with your daughter's best friend's mother?"

"I'm guilty of adultery. Not murder."

"Just curious. Did Gail mean anything to you?"

"That's nobody's business."

"I'm trying to learn more about your character. Was she your way of getting back at your wife? Or were your feelings for her deeper than you admit?"

"Okay, dammit. She melted my heart. I'll never forget her."

Sadler shuffled papers. "My notes say your wife never returned home after she asked a neighbor to watch Madison while she ran an errand. Police theorized you picked up Tanya on your way to your beach house. While you two were enjoying each other's company, Linda showed up and caught you and her best friend with your pants down, so to speak. During a heated argument, whether it was an accident or intentional, Linda ended up dead. Then you turned on Tanya because she witnessed what you did."

"That's the cops' theory. Gail was the only woman I saw that night."

"Then why was your wife's SUV found parked a hundred yards away?

"I've run that question through my mind a thousand times. I can't explain it."

After a long silence, Sadler asked, "I have a few questions for Danny to clarify, but police can't locate him. No employment records, tax returns, driver's license renewal, tickets, nothing."

"He often spoke of moving to Italy to help his father manage two restaurants in Venice."

"Do you remember the name of these restaurants?"

Roger shook his head. "Sorry, I don't."

Sadler scribbled notes on her pad. "I'll look into this further. Meanwhile, sit tight."

"Where the hell can I go, Detective?"

Chapter 3

Sadler returned a week later and asked Roger what he remembered about Gail's daughter.

"Little Jessica. A cute redhead. She and Madison were inseparable." A grin appeared on his face. "She had difficulty pronouncing my last name and called me Mr. Big Man."

"Jess isn't so little anymore. She's the game changer I spoke about earlier."

"You've had contact with Jess?"

Sadler nodded. "I've known her and her mom for a long time. Which is the reason I begged my captain to pull more strings than a puppeteer to convince the San Diego PD to work with me."

"Why didn't you tell me this sooner?"

"It's complicated."

"How are they?"

"Considering all that has happened, they're okay."

"What happened?"

"Three months ago, Jess began having recurring nightmares of a naked child, a naked man, and a fully clothed woman. The people in the dream are faceless. The two adults fought until the lady lay on the floor, not moving. She then heard a loud argument in another room that ended with another woman's screams. These dreams sent her to a psychiatrist. After putting her under hypnosis, the shrink determined Jess was the naked child, and she might have witnessed two murders."

"Oh my god. Linda's? Tanya's?"

"The shrink suggested Jess discuss the nightmares with her mother to see if an incident in her past could trigger her memory. With a little luck, she might recognize the name Jess heard the woman call out before he killed her."

"Whose name?"

"Someone Gail knew in her previous life."

Roger leaned forward. "Previous life? As in?"

"Gail had skeletons. This is when I stepped in and passed the information on to the San Diego PD. Thanks to their extensive research, we learned more about her ex-husband, why she left him, and of the man in Jessica's dreams."

"A suspect in the murders?"

"All we want to do is question him as of now." She shrugged her shoulders. "I spent a lot of time looking into events during the timeframe Gail lived in California. I read about the murders and learned police were looking for a Gail Vaughn to question her whereabouts that night. As I dug deeper, I discovered the homicide happened the same night Gail moved away. When she learned of your conviction, she swore she was with you until the wee hours of the morning and during the estimated time of death."

"Thank God! After twenty-six years, I have my alibi."

"Not so fast. I talked to Gail in-depth about Roger Brinkman. Considering it was only one night, she is very fond of you. Gail may lie as a favor for saving her daughter."

"You don't believe her?"

"It doesn't matter what I believe. Memories recovered under hypnosis are not admissible in a court of law. There isn't enough evidence for a retrial." She placed her hand on Roger's shoulder. "I'd give you Gail's contact info, but it's best not to give the D.A. any reason to claim you two collaborated on a story to free you from prison."

"How is Jessica holding up?"

"Jess is a tough broad. She's handling it in her own way." Sadler removed the vibrating phone from her back pocket. "I have to take this call. Excuse me."

Chapter 4

A half-hour later, Sadler returned with a hint of a smile. "The police have a suspect in custody. A U.S. Marshal is bringing him to California."

"The one who killed my wife and Tanya?"

"Yes. He confessed to everything."

"How did you find him?"

"It wasn't easy." Sadler paced the floor as she explained the chain of events that led to the death of two women. "Thirty years ago, four years before, your conviction, rape, and murder of twin seven-year-old girls belonging to a congressman in a wealthy section of Chicago monopolized the news media. A smudged partial fingerprint found on a necklace led police to a few suspects. One of those suspects, Tony Greco. A convicted pedophile and known *ghoster* affiliated with the Randazzo crime family in Chicago."

"Ghoster? As in one who sells identities of dead people not widely known?"

Sadler nodded. "Police did all they could to locate Greco, but his trail went cold. It wasn't until Gail came clean with her past. She admitted knowing him through her husband and turned to him for a new I.D."

"Why a new ID? Was she running from someone?"

"Are you familiar with mob boss Frankie Randazzo?"

"Who isn't? He's mentioned in the same breath as Capone."

"If Gail wishes to explain, she can, but I'll say no more, other than she pissed off Randazzo enough to run and hide from him."

"How does this Greco come into play with my wife's murder?"

Sadler exhaled enough air to inflate a balloon in one puff. "Eight months before your arrest, Gail left her husband and took with her a small storage box full of cash and a black book with names and contact info of her husband's associates. One of these associates was Tony Greco, who had changed his identity and moved to California when Chicago PD were closing in on him for the twin's murder. Desperate and having nowhere to run, she reached out to him for help."

"Why would she go to a pedophile with a young daughter to worry about?"

"She knew nothing of his sick sexual preferences. What she needed was new identification for her and her daughter. Not only did he help her with a new I.D., he offered his basement apartment until she grew comfortable being Gail Vaughn."

"What are you telling me? Tony Greco and Danny Jovino are the same person?"

"Do I have your attention now, Mr. Brinkman?"

"Danny in the mob? A pedophile? No way."

"It's true, and the reason Danny asked Gail to keep you company that night was so he could be alone with Jessica. During his watch, he treated the child to an ice cream soda, laced with Rohypnol."

"The date rape drug?"

Sadler nodded. "Given the proper dosage, it paralyzes the victim, making her unable to resist and impairs their memory." She reached into her purse for a Kleenex. "I'm too close to this case. What that bastard did to little Jess makes me want to vomit. A short time later, Danny's lover surprised him with a visit and caught him with Gail's naked toddler, his penis in a place it shouldn't be. After a violent confrontation, his mistress lay dead."

"Jessica's dream? The mystery woman was Tanya?"

"No, Mr. Brinkman. His lover was your wife. Tanya walked in a few minutes later and met the same fate when a fireplace poker crashed over her head."

"Linda and Danny?"

"This explains why he made the false, damaging statement about your affairs with Tanya. Intending to frame you for the murders, he stripped Tanya's clothing and drove to your beach house with the two corpses in the back of your wife's SUV. With a spare set of keys to your Mercedes on Linda's key chain, he dumped the dead women into your trunk while you and Gail were preoccupied. He then drove Linda's SUV home."

"My best friend hung me out to dry and let me take the fall for the murders?"

"He needed to cover his own ass. That's why Danny made up a story to have her leave California overnight. Before police questioned her.

"I understand her moving, but overnight? Just hours after spending time with me? Why so sudden?"

"Allow me to recount Danny's explanation and flash back twenty-six years."

***

Gail returned from her rendezvous a few hours before dawn. Danny greeted her as she pulled her car into the driveway. "You must leave California. And fast."

"Why? What's going on?"

"A friend from Chicago tipped me off. Frankie Randazzo is on his way. He knows you're staying with me."

He tossed two suitcases in the trunk, laid the groggy child into the back seat, and handed Gail a large envelope.

"What's this?"

"You are no longer Gail Vaughn. You're Kathy O'Shea from Seattle now. Paperwork and bio are inside. Read it when you get a chance. Drive as far from California as possible and never contact me again."

Roger had so many questions to ask, but words couldn't leave his lips.

"This is a lot to grasp, Mr. Brinkman. But there is so much more you need to learn."

"After hearing all these twists and turns, nothing would surprise me anymore."

"Wrong, Mr. Brinkman. More surprises are awaiting you. But before we continue, I'd like to finish with Danny's plan."

"Go ahead."

"After Gail sped off toward the interstate, Danny returned to your beach house with Linda's SUV. After waiting three hours for you to head home, he planted Tanya's bra under the pillow, her necklace on the floor, and hair fibers on the bed. Then walked to the railroad station a half-mile away. Before boarding the train, he dialed 911 from a payphone to report a stolen blue Mercedes carrying a large quantity of cocaine in the trunk, headed for the San Diego Freeway. He gave the license plate number and hung up before the operator asked any further questions."

Chapter 5

Sadler called in Zack to unlock the shackles that were a routine procedure when a prisoner enters the interrogation room. "I have a ton of paperwork to fill out. It shouldn't be long before the courts allow you to say goodbye to San Pelican State Prison. Your hell is almost over."

Tears clouded Roger's eyes. "I've waited half a lifetime for this day and never thought it would happen." He embraced Sadler and lifted her off the ground. After lowering her again, he apologized.

"That's okay. I needed a hug, too. We've both had a rough ride."

His voice cracked. "Do you think Madison will give me a chance to be a father again?"

"It'll take some adjusting from both parties, but once you sharpen your social skills, you and Madison can restart your lives and live happily ever after."

"Am I that crude?"

"I can't blame you for the chip on your shoulder after all you've gone through. It's no secret the company you've been hanging out with aren't the most polished people in the world." She threw him a wink. "This might sound awkward. Mom and I have invitations to an old friend's wedding. My husband is accompanying me. My mother has no date. She is your age, looks fabulous, and widowed. You two will make a good match. Interested?"

"Suppose we don't hit it off?"

"You guys have plenty to talk about. Mom's birth name is Maria. The ex-wife of a former henchman to the Randazzo crime family. She goes by Kathy O'Shea now." She winked, "For a short while, she used the name Gail Vaughn."

"Oh, my god! You're Jessica?"

She grinned. "It took you long enough to figure it out." She reached for his hands and squeezed them. "I'd like to introduce you to the bride before the big day, so you won't feel awkward at the ceremonies. We reconnected while I was working on this case. She and I were best friends during our early childhood. Madison can't wait to meet you." Detective Jessica

Bianco Vaughn O'Shea Sadler shed happy tears. "Welcome home, Mr. Big Man."

THE CALLER

Chapter 1

New Year's Eve

After quitting the habit last April, my resolve was never to have a cigarette touch my lips again. Yet the ashtray was full of smoked-down butts after I found an old pack of Virginia Slims during a cleaning frenzy this afternoon. I declined an invitation to join my girlfriends at the Times Square's New Year's Eve celebration, using my father's recent passing as an excuse. It had more to do with what happened on Cooper's Bridge last week.

The guilt of killing someone was bad enough, but the eyewitness in the truck had me scared to death. Did he see my face or read my license plate? Did the accident investigators find my shoe? All these questions beg for answers, which I got when the phone rang.

A week earlier, December 23

My nightmare began at Pierre Blanchard Cosmetics' annual Christmas party at the elegant Golden Pond. With hundreds of employees attending, my boss asked me to sit at the table with the representatives from A Scent of Paris. He needed my French language skills to put our guests at ease. My job was to sway them to accept the proposal Mr. Blanchard worked so hard on. If we are successful, my boss will consider me for the Marketing Manager position when Jack Bishop retires next spring.

The classy form-fitting red dress I wore to the party revealed more than enough cleavage and leg to draw attention. I sat with Mr. Blanchard, Jack Bishop, and the cosmetic giants from France, discussing how lucrative our marketing plan will be for both companies. Although the snowstorm forced our guests to leave early, I was confident we hadn't heard the last of Felipe and Raphael.

My private secretary joined me at the bar after my table cleared out. "How did it go, Renee?"

"Great, Vicki. When it's time to expand their market into North America, they'll know where to come."

"The two Frenchmen couldn't keep their eyes off you."

"Which is why Mr. Blanchard asked me instead of Michelle Beaumont, who never outgrew her training bra, to join them at their table."

"You think?" Vicki pointed toward the company's top mechanic. "Did you notice pathetic Herbicide parading around the room showing off his three-piece suit bought off the discount rack at Walmart?"

"Mr. Fashion, he's not. He'd shit if he knew my Christian Louboutin stilettos cost more than his entire wardrobe."

"Herb never noticed your shoes. The classless weasel gawked at you all night, focusing on other parts of your anatomy. It's obvious, girlfriend. He wants to stick his dipstick inside your high-powered engine." We shared laughs until Vicki mumbled, "Speak of the devil, here he comes."

"Dammit."

"Careful, Renee. You know how temperamental he is." As Herb approached, Vicki excused herself, leaving me stranded.

"The roads are a sheet of ice, Renee. You've had too much to drink. Leave your car here. Stay with me for the night."

"Good try, Herbert. Think of the gossip going around the office?"

"Who cares? It's nobody's business."

"Be real, Herb. We live different lifestyles. We're not even the same religion."

"Opposites attract. You're taller than me, but I'm large where it counts."

No way will I, Renee Pfeiffer, a company executive, and former swimsuit model hook up with a sleazy grease monkey. He should have known not to push the issue, but he refused to take no for an answer. Annoyed with his come-on, I snapped, "I know how to drive, dammit. Get out of my face."

I second-guessed my insensitive rejection as soon as his slouched body walked away and realized I should apologize. Screw him. Herb is a jerk. Next time he'll think twice before he comes on to me. Large where it counts? Give me a break.

I grabbed my purse and snuck out the back entrance. My remote starter set the BMW at a toasty temperature. When I got to my car, the defroster had already cleared my windows. I tossed my mink on the passenger seat and drove out of the parking lot.

Had I known the roads were this treacherous, I would have stayed at Vicki's. As cars played bumper cars on the slippery highway, I saw Herbicide's Hyundai following me in the rearview mirror. Traffic merged into one passable lane. Herb fell further behind. Heavy winds and blowing snow made visibility a challenge. Up ahead, around the next bend, was the Lakeshore Drive exit. He wouldn't see me get off two exits earlier than usual. Dumb Herbicide will continue toward Waterside Marina, unaware I had turned off.

As I approached the narrow bridge that crossed the lake, I passed a small white car with the driver's door open, embedded in a snowbank. I continued another five hundred feet before I reached the narrow bridge that had no lighting. As I drove across, I put on my hi-beams just in time to see a stationary truck in the middle of the bridge. Too late to hit my brakes, knowing I'd skid on the icy surface and run into the vehicle. So, I took my foot off the gas pedal, held the steering wheel tight, and hugged the wall, hoping I'd squeeze by. Just as I got parallel to the truck, I saw a dark figure appear on my right. I had no place to swerve.

THUD!

I tapped the brakes and coasted to a stop. My trembling hands fumbled for the flashlight in the glove box—a flashlight with a low battery. I exited my car and shuffled my feet to keep my balance while walking on the icy surface. As I approached the center of the bridge, the truck drove away. *Where the hell is he going?*

A sneaker lay next to what looked like blood stains soaked into the snow. I followed footsteps to the railing and aimed my flickering flashlight below. I screeched in horror at the silhouette of a human figure floating face down in the water.

SHIT. What have I done?

An approaching snowplow told me to not hang around any longer. I impulsively kicked the bloody sneaker into the lake. As my right leg swung forward, my stiletto flew off my foot, landing somewhere in a snowdrift. I searched in vain for it, but my flickering flashlight flickered for the last time. Hearing crunching snow and ice from a nearby snowplow, I skated to my car and drove away, unable to retrieve my shoe.

Chapter 2

I pulled into my garage and checked for damages. Deep scratches, a broken headlight, a missing side-view mirror, and a cracked grill. Not to mention the bloodstains and the victim's frozen baseball cap wedged between the bumper. Accident investigators will identify BMW car parts. If they find my Christian Louboutin, they'll search for a woman driver with my shoe size.

I collapsed on the couch and cried myself to sleep. When I woke up three hours later, I second-guessed my decision to leave the scene of a fatal accident. A tragic mistake, but I can't undo what I did. Turning myself in would ruin me. The best I could do was cover my tracks before police checked local body shop receipts for BMW repairs. After a strong cup of coffee, I worked on a strategy to save my ass. Herb was my ace in the hole.

Not being a Christian, Christmas meant little to him. Although a lowlife, his reputation as a mechanic and body tech was legendary. I recently heard of his part-time business in his garage. It was time to put my acting skills to work and perform an Academy Award performance as I sweet-talk the jerk into fixing the damages. I'd pay him cash and ask for no invoice that would leave any trace of having my car repaired. After I mistreated him at the party, I wouldn't blame him if he told me to play in traffic. But I know Herb well enough. He will never walk away from a big payday. Nor would he ignore the sight of half of me hanging out of my low-cut sweater worn for the occasion.

The GPS took me to a run-down house. Herb not only looked and acted like white trash, but he also lived like it. Despite how cold it was, I left my coat on the front passenger seat to allow horny Herbicide to get a peek at paradise.

"Renee? You're the last person I'd expect to be knocking on my front door."

The gaze in his eyes and bulge in his pants told me he had no intentions of turning me away.

"I apologize for my behavior last night. Alcohol makes me run off my mouth."

"Apology accepted. How 'bout we cuddle in front of the fireplace with a bottle of wine and see where it goes?"

"Slow down, Herb. I don't jump into the sack with just anyone."

"I'm not just anybody. Give me a chance to prove it."

"Bad timing, Herb. I have too much on my plate right now. Not only am I dealing with my dad's recent death, but the accident I had last night has me upset. I'm pissed, Herb. My car is a mess."

"Accident?"

"On my way home from the party, I hit a deer on Beaver Creek Road. My Beemer looks like crap. I was hoping you could fix the damages before I drive to New Jersey to sort out my late father's finances."

"Let's check it out," he said as he went outside to examine the front end. "No structural damage. Touchup paint and a good detail job will be easy. With suppliers closed for the holidays, getting the replacement parts I'll need is another story. But my chop shop connections can dig up what we need." He paused for a second. "This won't be a cheap fix. File an accident report. Let your insurance company pay for it."

"And have rates go through the roof and wait a week before repairs begin? No thanks. Just do your magic. Fix the damn car. I'll pick it up this evening."

"Impossible. This baby needs hours of work, and the paint needs time to dry. The best I can do is have it ready by late afternoon tomorrow. And that's pushing it."

"Then push it. No sense standing around bullshitting."

"The White Whale?"

"Huh?"

"The White Whale. Quiet, romantic, and great food. Pricey, but I take care of my girlfriends."

"Ah, how sweet. I've eaten there. I love the ambiance and soft piano music. You have good taste." Not wanting to linger on his dinner proposal, I said, "Herb? The car?"

He motioned to his garage. "Pull it inside."

I took a cab home and returned late the following afternoon dressed in jeans and a bulky turtleneck sweater. No more free peekaboo for Herbicide. As I stepped from the cab, I saw my BMW looking immaculate. The car was in showroom condition.

Herb greeted me as I walked up the driveway. He noted the extra time he took to clean the deer's blood residue off the windshield. Having no problems with his quality of workmanship, I paid the bill in cash and thanked Herb for a job well done. But I came short of giving him a well-deserved hug. He's called Herbicide for a reason. No hugs for him. Not today. Not ever.

On the way home, a state trooper pulled behind me. When I turned right at the light, he followed. I checked my speed. All was good. Wanting to get him off my tail, I was careful to put on my directional before changing lanes. I watched in the rearview mirror as he also changed lanes. Even though I hate Starbucks coffee, I turned into the parking lot, hoping to get him off my tail. Instead, he tailgated me with his lights flashing and siren wailing. I was having an anxiety attack as I parked in the first available space. My heart pounded as the officer walked toward me. "License and registration, ma'am."

I searched through my purse. *Stay calm, Renee. Relax. Don't give signals that could arouse suspicion.* "Did I do anything wrong, officer?"

"Not sure yet." He examined my front end before returning to his squad car to call it in.

Minutes later, he handed me my information back. "Sorry for the inconvenience, Ms. Pfeiffer. Just a routine check. A young woman surfaced in Cooper's Lake early this morning. An apparent hit-and-run. It's all over the news."

"How awful, officer. Any witnesses?"

"None have stepped up so far. Accident investigators found broken grill parts, a mangled side-view mirror, and an expensive hi-heel at the scene. Police are looking for a female driver in a red BMW."

"Oh, my! I hope you don't think I had anything to do with this."

"You're clean. Your car shows no sign of damage. I see no reason to question you further."

"Any chance of an out-of-state driver?"

"It's possible. But if the police don't apprehend this perp before the deceased family does, may God help her. The victim was crime boss Carmine Levitino's teenage daughter. This could get ugly if the Mob finds her first." He touched the brim of his hat. "Have a Merry Christmas."

He left in pursuit of another red BMW that had just driven by.

Chapter 3

A week later,

Alone in my townhouse on New Year's Eve, I watched the countdown on television as the ball made its descent. Cameras zoomed in on a half-million people cheering in the New Year. *Auld Lang Syne* played in the background.

I lowered the volume to answer the ringing phone, expecting it to be my girlfriend. I masked my depression and answered in a cheerful voice, "Happy New Year."

"Happy for some," a muffled voice answered. "Not for Loretta's family."

"Who is this?"

"She had so much to live for until you ran her off Cooper's Bridge."

My body went limp, my knees felt like rubber. "Wrong number. I haven't driven on that bridge in years."

"Bullshit. And I'm sure you know by now; the victim was Mafia Godfather Carmine Levitino's teenage daughter."

"Go to hell!"

"Compensate me for my silence, or you're the one going to hell when Levitino gets his hands on you."

"You have nothing on me. I'll call the police if you harass me again."

"Unlikely. I recorded your accident on my dashcam. After Levitino's boys shake down your mechanic friend who repaired your car, the wimp will spill the beans."

"What are you talking about?"

"How's this sound? Your red BMW crossed Cooper's Bridge at a quarter to three. You wore a sexy red dress with matching stilettos. One of which you left behind. So cut the shit. Stop denying it and get down to business. We need to agree on a solution we can both live with."

I remained quiet.

"Still there, Renee?"

"Goodbye, asshole!" I slammed down the receiver.

Thirty seconds later, the phone rang again. This time, I allowed the call to go to the answering machine.

"Big mistake, Renee. I'm trying to save your life. Show your appreciation. If you don't pick up the phone, I'll pay a visit to Levitino and give him everything he needs to revenge his daughter's death. You can't run from this. You killed a mafia princess. Papa bear won't take this lightly. Pick up the damn phone and hear me out. Let's make a deal."

I picked up the receiver. "What do you want?"

"Match the fifty grand reward money. Take care of me, or Levitino will take care of you. I'm the lesser of two evils."

"I don't have fifty thousand dollars."

"Crying poverty won't work. With your salary, you gotta have money stashed away. Calculate how much your life is worth. Think about this. You won't be so pretty after Levitino finishes with you. Women who die a slow and painful death never are."

"What's saying this won't be the first installment of a lifetime payment plan?"

"You have my word. Hold up your end of the deal, and you'll never hear from me again. If you don't get your head out of your ass by the end of this phone call, you'll wish you were never born."

Mid-April...

I left a duffel bag full of money at a vacant windmill on Serenity Drive four months ago. With that dark side of my life behind me, I awaited the opportunity of a lifetime. Mr. Blanchard asked me to head the presentation when representatives from A Scent of Paris returned to America with their CEO, Mathieu Dupont. If I could do my magic, Pierre Blanchard would attain exclusive rights for their cosmetics line in North America.

I rehearsed my sales pitch while waiting for Mr. Blanchard and his clients to return from the airport. The white business suit I chose for the occasion was not as revealing as the red dress from the Christmas party. But still provocative enough to keep the Frenchmen interested. Most company employees punched out for lunch, but my dedicated secretary hung around if I needed anything.

"Excuse the interruption, Renee," Vicki said as she paged me on my private line. "I have someone on the phone. He insists he speaks to you. I explained you'd be entering a meeting shortly. He said the call would be a brief one. He claims it's important. Wanted to run it by you before I tell him you're unavailable."

"I have a few minutes. Put me through."

Vicki nodded, "Line seven."

"Hello, Renee Pfeiffer speaking. How may I help you?"

"Hello, Lady in Red."

I gasped in horror. "You promised never to contact me again."

"I never expected Levitino to double his reward."

"Fuck you."

"Sounds good to me. But let's discuss our bedroom rendezvous at a later date."

"You won't get another nickel from me or anything else."

The caller raised his voice. "You're not in the position to negotiate."

"I don't have another fifty-grand."

"You got till the weekend to find it." He hung up before I could reply.

I fought back the tears. Vicki buzzed me. Mr. Blanchard and the representatives from A Scent of

Paris had arrived. They were waiting for me in the conference room.

Disturbed by the phone call, I lost all concentration. My rehearsed presentation turned into a disaster when I left my reference notes on my desk and mangled my French. Not to mention mixing up Felipe and Raphael's names. After exchanging cold handshakes with the CEO, Mr. Dupont promised to get back to Mr. Blanchard, but his body language told us differently.

Our client's limousine hadn't left the parking lot when my boss called me into his office and shut the door. In a stern voice said, "I expected more from you. You came preoccupied and unprepared. You haven't been the Renee Pfeiffer I know since Christmas. What on earth is going on?"

"I'll work it out, Mr. Blanchard."

"You better. Until further notice, you'll be working in Human Resources under Michelle Beaumont. Paula Tucker will replace you in marketing."

"Is my job in jeopardy?"

"Only you can answer that. Cross over that bridge and confront your problem head-on. Resolve it and fast. I'm giving you the rest of the week off. Do what you need to do to rid yourself of the demons tearing your insides apart. Return to work Monday morning refreshed, with your head on your shoulders."

The cliché, *cross over the bridge,* hit me like a hammer. Mr. Blanchard was right. I need to confront the problem head-on. But how? A drunk driver leaving a fatal accident scene couldn't go to the police. And I couldn't afford to pay off the caller again, nor will I look over my shoulder for the rest of my life.

The following morning, my thoughts were to uncork a bottle of wine and drown my sorrows, which would only add to my problems. My excessive drinking got me into this mess. I needed a clear head to explain my side of the story. Will he forgive me and respect my decision to come forward? Or will he be so crazed that he'd torture me and turn my white business suit into a bloody red one?

"Oh, God, I can't believe I'm thinking of doing this? Have I lost my mind? The Mafia plays by their own rules. What I'm about to do could be the last mistake I ever make. I had to try something, even if it killed me."

I searched through my walk-in closet and removed a white business suit I bought just last week. It felt comfortable when I tried it on in the store, but I never saw myself in the mirror wearing it.

"Damn it," I grunted. "I had no idea how the fabric clung to my every curve. Should I change into something less eye-catching and dress with a pair of cut-off jeans and a baggy T-shirt? No, that wouldn't work. Levitino would respect me more if I were dressed like a professional." I sighed. "Here goes nothing."

***

I swore to never take this route again. Yet, I just drove over the infamous bridge that changed my life four months ago. This time it wasn't snowing, nor was it the criminal returning to the crime scene. I turned left on Sea View Court, a road few people travel except friends and acquaintances of mob boss Carmine Levitino.

At the end of the block, overlooking a private beach, stood a large, well-kept Victorian surrounded by a security gate. Whoever said crime doesn't pay hasn't seen this fortress.

Before reaching my destination, I pulled off the road to let my practical side talk me out of what I was about to do. It didn't.

I stepped from the car and walked to the security gate. Frankie or Tony, Vito, or Sal, or whoever approached me. "Can I help you, sweetheart?"

"I'd like to speak to Mr. Levitino, please."

"Sorry. My boss accepts no unscheduled visitors."

"He'll want to listen to what I have to say."

"I'll relay the message. What is it?"

"I must tell him myself. In private."

"I can't allow anyone through the gate."

"Then who can? It's important."

"That would be our security chief. But you'd rather not deal with Gino. He can be unpleasant when people show up unannounced."

"Get him. Please." The guard called Gino on his cell. He walked away so I wouldn't hear what he said, but I have excellent hearing. "Gino. I have a dynamite-looking babe at the front gate. She wants to meet with Carmine. I told her she couldn't see him, but she won't take no for an answer."

The guard clipped his cell to his hip holster flipped and told me, "Gino will be with you in a minute."

"It wasn't long before a muscular man limped over. His eyes examined me from head to toe. "What do ya want, lady? People don't drop in around here without notice. Who sent you?"

"Nobody."

"Unannounced guests ain't welcome. What's your business? You a reporter?"

"I work for a cosmetic firm, but my visit has nothing to do with my occupation."

"My boss has cosmetic connections. He's not interested in any crap you're selling."

"I'm not selling anything, sir. I just want to talk to him."

"Fat chance of that happening." He opened his jacket to reveal his gun. "My boss has no time for you."

"Run it by him. Let him decide."

"The odds of me allowing you past the front gate are the same as winning the lottery."

"I'm not armed." I held my arms out. "Search me, dammit. Get your jollies if it turns you on."

I tolerated the pervert's roaming hands, expecting his inspection to be more thorough than necessary. The prick got his feels in and found nothing that would make me a threat. "I'll pass along your information. If my boss has time to meet with you next century, I'll be in touch."

"Why search me if I can't see him now?"

Before he could answer, Gino's cell phone rang. I could only hear his side of the conversation. "I'll get rid of her, Carmine." He looked up at the balcony at someone with thick salt and pepper hair viewing us with binoculars. "It's for your safety. Gimme time to check her background. She claims she works in cosmetics, but who knows what her game is." He voiced his disapproval before he hung up and attached his cell to his belt clip. "Follow me, Blondie."

Chapter 4

As Gino led me up the stairs, he gave a stern warning. "Not sure what's up your sleeve, but flashing a monster set of tits won't mean shit to my boss. He's a busy man. He has no time to listen to your sales pitch. You're lucky if he gives you three minutes before throwing your ass out the fuckin' door."

Saying no more, he led me to an office twice the size of Pierre Blanchard's conference room. Mr. Levitino kissed the back of my hand. "It's an honor to have such a beautiful woman wanting to meet me."

"You will soon learn how ugly I am."

"Impossible." He turned to his guard. "That'll be all, Gino. I got this."

"I'll hang around, Boss. Just in case."

"She doesn't look dangerous. And your thorough search proves she's clean."

"It's not every day a broad comes here to talk to you. I have bad vibes from her."

"Whatever the reason, I'm curious. I'll call if needed."

The notorious mobster asked me to sit next to a mahogany desk that centered the room. He continued to stand. The elegant office had expensive artwork on the walls. A crystal chandelier hung from a cathedral ceiling. A digital picture frame sat on top of a wine rack full of bottles not sold at Walmart. The large window behind a marble bar looked out at the same lake that took his daughter.

"Is that your red BMW parked in front of the gate?"

"Yes, sir."

"I prefer black cars myself, although I've had an interest in red Beemer's since Christmas."

My heart pounded. Levitino suspects something.

"I'd love to take a spin with you, but it's not healthy for a high-level target to drive in a car like yours. I can't go anywhere without bodyguards and bulletproof vehicles."

"As glorious as your life appears, it's a shame you can't enjoy the simple pleasures. When have you last walked through the park or gone to a ballgame?"

"A long time ago. It's the price I pay for being who I am. But nothing matters anymore. My daughter's death has left a hole in my heart. I have money and power, but I'd give it all up to have her back." He cleared his throat. "I assume you heard of Loretta's misfortune last winter."

A lump formed in my throat. Coming here was suicidal. Sensing Levitino's grief, asking for forgiveness was not an option. I wasn't getting out of here alive. A guard stood at the gate, and Gino was waiting to get his hands on me again. There is no way out.

He headed toward the wine rack. "You look uneasy. I have just the medicine to calm your nerves. Red or white?"

"No preference, sir."

"Red might be best for the occasion." He showed me the label—one of my favorite Italian wines. "I've saved this bottle for the right moment. This is as good a time as ever to pop the cork." He poured two tall glasses. We clinked to a toast. "To a brave woman with the courage to do what's right."

"I don't understand. You don't know why I'm here."

"Let's cut to the chase, Ms. Pfeiffer. Is your visit related to what happened on Cooper's Bridge last winter?"

I looked down, avoiding eye contact as my body trembled. *He knows.*

His fingers lifted my chin. "If there was any doubt about your mission today, your guilt-ridden face convinced me you aren't the Avon lady."

"It was an accident." Tears dripped down my cheeks as I bawled like a baby. "I came here to ask for your forgiveness. I won't get it, will I?"

Levitino handed me a linen handkerchief from his suit jacket pocket. "These four months must have been hell for you, Ms. Pfeiffer."

"Yes, it's been hell, but I can't imagine what you've gone through. And it's my fault. I'd give anything for it to be me instead of your daughter. I can't live with the guilt anymore. But how can you forgive me for letting her drown without doing a damn thing to help?"

"Loretta didn't drown. An autopsy report found no water in her lungs. She was dead before she hit the water."

My pleading eyes locked onto his. "An apology won't bring your daughter back. I can't undo all that has happened. If you can't forgive me, please, at least make it quick and painless."

"You must think I'm a monster."

"Your notoriety speaks for itself. I've watched enough gangster movies and how the mob attains justice. An eye for an eye. Is that how my life will end?"

He positioned his hands on my shoulders, inches from my throat. I froze in place. *Will he strangle me?*

"Don't believe everything you see in the movies. I don't work that way."

"What way do you work? Is there something worse than death? Why not take your gun out of the desk drawer and get this over with?"

"What makes you believe there's a gun in the desk drawer?"

"A man like you must protect himself."

"A man like me? Understand this. I had my back turned to you when I looked out at the lake while you sat near my desk. I didn't become who I am for lack of caution. In this business, you trust no one. If a gun were in the drawer, I wouldn't let you anywhere near it." He removed a pistol from a holster inside his jacket. "Like my American Express card. Never leave home without it." He winked. "I'm not always at my desk."

My heart pounded. *This is it. A bullet to the head. At least it will be quick.* He aimed the barrel toward the ceiling and emptied the bullets into his hand. He held them in front of my face. "Count them. Six slugs." He placed the shells in his pocket and tucked his gun back into his vest holster.

"Now we're on the same playing field. Talk to me."

"About what?"

"Start at the beginning. Tell me exactly what happened on the bridge that night."

"Why ask for a detailed description of your daughter's death? It's hard enough for me to think about it. Your daughter is dead. I killed her. Hearing the details will break your heart."

"My heart shattered in pieces the day Loretta died. It can't break more than it already has. Tell me everything, Ms. Pfeiffer. Don't leave out even the smallest detail, no matter how meaningless it may seem."

I told him about the party, why I took the detour and the truck that caused me to drive close to the wall. "The visibility was terrible. With it dark on the bridge and your daughter wearing dark clothing, I didn't see her until it was too late." I avoided eye contact when I mentioned the bloody sneaker and human figure floating in the lake.

"It took a brave woman to come here today. I admire your courage and principles."

"If I were so damn brave, then why did it take me four months to confess? I can't run away from this any longer. The guilt, nightmares, loss of sleep, and dealing with …" I paused, and with sad eyes, mumbled, "Never mind. It's got nothing to do with you."

"I'll decide on that, Renee. What are you dealing with?"

"It's a personal issue."

"Talk to me. What's going on?"

"Your daughter's killer is in the same room as you. Why are you so calm and understanding?"

"It was a hit-and-run, Renee. You hit. You ran. You've been running since. If you knew the truth, it wouldn't have taken so long to come forward." He pointed toward the lake. "Whatever happened on that bridge is still a mystery. But, with your help, we could be one step closer to the answer."

"What mystery? What answer? I already confessed. The search is over. According to you, it has just begun. Why?"

"Sometimes we take situations at face value and don't recognize they are not what they seem."

"Mr. Levitino. Where are you going with this? What am I missing?"

"Ever hear the cliché, *can't see the forest for the trees*?"

"It's when someone is so deeply involved in the details of a problem. They fail to visualize the obvious and can't see what's in front of their eyes."

"Exactly."

"What is it I didn't see?"

"It's not what you didn't see. It's what you saw but not aware you saw it." Levitino paused, waiting for me to respond. I didn't. All I could do was cry. "Allow me to give my take on this, Ms. Pfeiffer. The reason you came here today is deeper than the guilt of what happened to Loretta. Something else in your personal life has turned your world upside down. You don't know how to deal with it. Correct me if I'm wrong."

"You're very perceptive."

"I'm a good listener. Let me help."

"Why help me?"

"I have my reasons. What's going on?"

"An eyewitness to the accident is blackmailing me to pay for his silence. Now he's asking for more."

"The truck driver?"

"I doubt it. The caller said he had the accident recorded on his dashcam. With the truck facing the opposite direction, it's unlikely he could have recorded it. I'm thinking the driver of the snowplow?"

"Whoever it is, I don't like him capitalizing on my daughter's death." Levitino paced the floor. "Loretta wore a plaid skirt, a beige sweater, white knee-high leather boots, and a white ski jacket the day she died. So much for your theory of her wearing dark clothing and sneakers."

"It happened so fast, but I know I saw a figure in dark clothing. If your daughter wore boots, where did the sneaker come from?"

"That's the sixty-four-thousand-dollar question. I'm offering an even higher reward for the answer."

Chapter 5

"Mr. Levitino? What aren't you telling me?"

"Let's start with this. Police found Loretta's abandoned Miata on the side of the road, just before Cooper's Bridge. Her door ajar, keys still in the ignition."

"Yes. I remember passing it."

"She'd go nowhere without her purse, cell phone, or the pistol I insisted she carry at all times. None of these items were at the scene or in her Miata. It was near zero degrees that night. Why was her ski jacket unbuttoned? Why wasn't she wearing panties? The medical examiner's office claimed her clothes wouldn't have torn the way they did from the impact of a collision." Levitino cleared his throat. "She was running from a sexual attack. Whoever did this may have run her over purposely. Clear your guilt. The person you hit on the bridge was Loretta's killer after he tossed her over the bridge. You may have injured him, but he somehow drove away."

"Are you kidding me? If I had known, I would have stepped forward sooner."

"You didn't know, Renee. I'm just sorry you went through so much drama. Your memory was foggy. You drank too much at the party and were not alert. Your imagination played tricks on you. In your deeper subconscious, you saw something that could lead us to Loretta's killer. We need to find out what it is."

"I told you everything I remember."

Levitino rested his hand on my shoulder. "How often do we save a file on a computer and can't find it later? Think of your brain as a hard drive. You stored the information somewhere. We just have to open the right folder."

I pointed to my head. "If that's the case, my hard drive never saved it."

"It's saved somewhere. We'll find it." He ran his fingers through his salt and pepper hair. The sadness in his eyes showed the emptiness in his heart. "Help me out here. I need you." He rubbed the back of his neck. "In my profession, the threat of retaliation from a rival is always a concern. I called for an emergency gathering with the Commission and met with the

Bosses. All the families assured me there were no internal disputes I wasn't aware of."

"Mr. Levitino. I'm so sorry, but I told you everything."

He pounded his right fist into the palm of his left hand. This is the first time during my visit that he displayed anger. "Dammit! Think hard. Play the scene back in your mind. Give me something---anything."

"It most likely means nothing, but the victim's baseball cap got stuck in the grill. I tossed it into the fireplace to destroy the evidence, just in case. Navy blue with a red 'B' in ornate lettering on it."

He strolled over to the digital picture frame to tap the forward arrow until he paused at a couple standing together. "Loretta and Gino, last summer. Did the hat look like the one Gino is wearing?"

"Yes, the same hat."

"Boston Red Sox. Gino is a huge Red Sox fan. That narrows down our search to about ten million people."

"Oh, my god. Mr. Levitino? The truck parked in the background. It looks the same as the one on the bridge."

"Truck? That's an SUV."

"What's the difference?"

The door flew open. Gino burst in, aiming a gun at Levitino. "It took you long enough to figure it out. Now, put your piece on the bar. Step back against the window."

Levitino did as ordered. "Why, Gino? We treated you like family. You and Loretta were as close as brother and sister."

"She could have been more than a sister, but Daddy would disapprove. She was too good for me."

"Damn straight she was. You treat women like crap. You're also twice her age."

"That's the problem, Carmine. Loretta couldn't take a shit without your permission."

"If you had a problem with me, why take it out on Loretta? She didn't deserve it."

"Your sweet little angel turned out to be an asshole, just like Daddy." Gino removed Levitino's gun from the bar and fired a bullet into his boss's kneecap, dropping him to the floor.

"Shit!" I cried as I rushed over to the wounded Mafia Don. I placed my hand on Mr. Levitino's shoulder. Lost for words, all I could say was, "I'm sorry to get you in the middle of this."

Gino yelled, "You should be sorry, bitch. If you hadn't driven over Cooper's Bridge that night, none of us would be in this dire situation."

"How can you do this to him? Hasn't he suffered enough?"

"Suffer? You ain't seen nothing yet. Daddy is gonna feel Loretta's pain, cry her tears, and taste her blood. Then after I break his heart with the details of the last minutes of his precious daughter's life, I'll blow his fuckin' brains out."

Levitino groaned and held his hands over his knee. "Somehow, you'll pay for this, you bastard."

Gino laughed. "It'll never happen. This is your final curtain. Your show is over."

"Leave him alone," I shouted. "How can you be so vicious?"

"Shut the hell up, Blondie. Get back behind the desk where I can see you, or I'll deflate your balloons with my next two bullets."

Gino meant business, and I did what the evil bastard said. I wasn't getting out of here alive unless I somehow overpowered him. But that would be next to impossible. Gino had a physique like Hercules. But I had to think of something fast.

Gino continued. "Loretta heard rumors at a Christmas party about the fourteen-year-old Honduran whore I won in a poker game and kept chained in my basement."

"Fourteen?" Levitino grunted. "She's only a child."

"No big deal. As a trafficking victim since she was seven years old, it's the only life she knows. She experienced, and her grownup tits are as large as Loretta's. So, don't classify her as a child. Instead of going straight home after the party, Loretta took a detour to my place to question the rumors. I told her it was none of her business. She pulled a pistol from her purse. She said it was her business and wouldn't think twice about pulling the trigger. The bitch marched me downstairs at gunpoint. She took her eyes off me for a split second when she saw my naked Chiquita Banana chained to the wall. I lunged at her. We wrestled. I got possession of the gun and pistol-whipped her face."

"May you rot in hell, you prick."

"You'll be there first, Carmine. Like in five minutes from now."

Carmine fought with the pain as he attempted to stand, but his leg injury hampered his mobility.

"Don't even try it. My next bullet goes between your eyes." Gino continued. "I ripped the buttons off her sweater and unclipped her front hook bra before yanking off her panties. I was all set to do the deed. She lifts her knee. Bullseye! Right in my fuckin nuts. She pushed me off and ran upstairs to her car without her purse. I chased her Miata until it slid into a snowbank. She tried to escape on foot but slipped on the ice near the center of the bridge. I kept driving until I ran the cunt over."

Levitino moaned.

"I made a U-turn and pulled up next to her still conscious mangled body." He grabbed his crotch. "I wanted to do her right there, but it was too fuckin' cold and didn't want to leave any DNA inside her. But her smoking hot body was just what I needed to warm my hands. She looked me straight in the eyes when I squeezed her grapefruits. Her nipples stiffened. I cupped her left tit in the palm of my hand. I felt her last heartbeat."

Levitino shouted multiple curse words.

"I tossed her dead body over the railing, into the lake. Then here comes Barbie Doll in her BMW. I crouched down against the sidewall. The bitch sideswipes me. I'll walk with a limp for the rest of my life. As brilliant as you are, you believed I tore up my knee helping an old lady stuck in a snowdrift. And then you sent me a get-well card while I recuperated from my knee surgery."

"You'll never get away with it, Gino. But whatever you do, don't hurt Renee?"

"She part of my plan. There were gunshots. I rushed in to see the broad holding your Smith & Wesson. She aimed the gun at me. I reacted faster and emptied my Magnum into your assassin. Afterward, I'll place your gun in her hand and fire the remaining bullets into your already dead body. Gunpowder residue will show she fired the gun."

Gino kept his focus on his boss, yet he directed his comments at me. "I recognized your car and sexy body the second I saw you. Same broad who damn near killed me on the bridge that night." He aimed Levitino's Smith & Wesson at his boss. "Goodbye." He pulled the trigger three times. Click. Click. Click. Gino tossed the empty weapon aside and took aim with his loaded Magnum.

Four loud explosions filled the room. Two hit the gangster, dropping him to the floor.

Chapter 6

Frozen in place, I looked down at the body lying at my feet, the smoking gun still clutched in my hands. Gino lay motionless on the floor. Gino's blood splattered all over my white business suit, but better his blood than mine. Levitino crawled over to pry my fingers from the weapon. He checked Gino's pulse.

"Is he dead?"

"Not yet, Renee." He aimed the gun three inches from Gino's heart and pulled the trigger. More blood splattered on Levitino and me. "He is now." Carmine then asked, "I told you there was no gun in my desk drawer. Thank God you had the foresight to look for one, anyway."

"Maybe I watch too many gangster movies, Mr. Levitino. But what I don't understand is you emptied your bullets earlier. You showed me six shells. Where did the bullet Gino shoot you with come from?"

"Smith & Wesson, model 686 holds seven rounds, not six."

"Why leave one bullet?"

"I said earlier, in this business, you trust nobody. I was confident your intentions were on the level, but I needed a security blanket just in case." He dialed a number in his contacts. "Go home, Renee. You were never here. Nor were you on the bridge that night. I called Sal at the front gate. He's on his way up to get me to the hospital. He also left the front gate open. Go now. You have clearance to leave. No questions asked."

"You're not what I expected, Mr. Levitino."

"I'll take that as a compliment. Now, get out of here."

***

Sunday afternoon, a black Cadillac pulled into my driveway. Mr. Levitino eased out of the backseat, walking with a cane. Two bodyguards stood outside while his chauffeur remained behind the wheel. Escorting Mr. Levitino to my front door and carrying two duffle bags was the one who Carmine called to bring him to the hospital. I welcomed them inside.

Levitino introduced me to Sal. "You remember, Renee? The bravest woman I've ever met."

"And a beautiful one as well," Sal answered as he laid the duffle bags at my feet. "No need to count it. It's all there."

"What's all there?"

"The caller won't be needing your money anymore."

"My gosh. Gino was the caller?"

"No, Ms. Pfeiffer. He wasn't."

"If not, who was?"

Levitino answered, "You've seen enough gangster movies. You know not to ask questions. My men took care of the problem. You need not worry anymore."

"Why two duffle bags?"

"The extra money wouldn't fit inside one."

"What extra money?"

"Do the math. When my boys visited the blackmailer, they recovered a little more than half the blackmail money you paid. Add this to the one hundred-thousand-dollar reward money for identifying Loretta's killer. Add up the numbers, Renee. One hundred thirty thousand dollars."

"No, no, no. I can't accept a reward."

"Yes, you will. When a man like me makes an offer you can't refuse- you better take it."

"Mr. Levitino? You've already ...."

"Don't Mr. Levitino me, Renee. It's Carmine. If you have any problem being on a first-name basis, I'll fit you for cement shoes. Size eight, right?" He broke out in laughter. "Come over here. We can both use a hug."

＊＊

The reward money did not stop there. Like most good friends with connections, he helped me land a sweet contract with an Italian cosmetic company. A deal that more than compensated for the Scent of Paris fiasco opportunity I screwed up. Because of it, I got the promotion when Jack Bishop retired.

It took me months to build up the nerve to ask Carmine for an answer to a question that always bothered me. Since we were like family now, I felt he wouldn't be as secretive to me anymore. "Please, Carmine, after what we've gone through together, I need to know the truth. Was Gino already dead when you fired the extra bullet into his heart?"

"It takes a certain person to kill someone, Renee. You are not that person."

"You didn't answer my question. Was Gino alive when you...?"

"Of course. Why else would I shoot him?"

I'm not sure if Carmine was telling the truth, nor did he mention the blackmailer's fate. But when Herb never showed up at work again, I wondered.

Printed in Great Britain
by Amazon

77062724R00161